I0594353

# KEEPING KATIE

## THE MAPLE RIDGE SERIES

STELLA QUINN

JELLY
J FISH
PRESS

The moral right of the author has been asserted. No part of this book may be reproduced, stored in a retrieval system, or transmitted by any means, electronic, mechanical, by photocopier or scanner or upload, without the prior written consent of the author.

This is a work of fiction. While the locations in this book are a mixture of real and imagined, the characters are totally fictitious. Any resemblance to actual people living or dead is entirely coincidental.

© Copyright 2020 Stella Quinn Author

All rights reserved.
A Jellyfish Press Book
ISBN trade paperback 978 06486935-5-0
ISBN largeprint paperback 978 06486935-6-7

## A NOTE FROM THE AUTHOR
### ROMANCE | ADVENTURE | ESCAPE

Romance, adventure and escape are the themes I love in romance novels.

I'm also a big fan of dogs in romance … hence my involvement in this series of cozy mysteries. The fabulous team at Sweet Promise Press publish this series in ebook format as the Gold Coast Retrievers series, and there are 14 available as I write this (July 2020). Jellyfish Press publishes the paperback format of these stories as the Maple Ridge Series.

*Keeping Katie* is my first contribution to this series.

*Vexing Veronica* is the second.

If you enjoy these, why not try my other series?

**The Island Escape Series** began with an idea about three friends, all of them unlucky in love, escaping on a faraway adventure and finding a holiday romance that turns into their happy ever after.

Those three friends are Charlotte, Sabrina and Antonia, who are totally unalike except for the bond of friendship they share.

The first three novels in this series won awards: Tropic Storm, Stowaway and Island Fling.

The series now includes a prequel, a Christmas novella and a short story or two, and I'm always looking for new island ideas for the next novel.

**The Clementine Springs Series** moves far, far away from tropical islands to a pretty lakeside town in the foothills of the Adirondacks on the border of New York State and Vermont.

Eccentric characters, heroes you want to snuggle with under a blanket by the fire, heroines who learn to live and love again in all that clear mountain air ... there's a lot to adore in this growing series. The novella, *The Umbrella Diaries* is a great place to start reading about the wonderful people of Clementine Springs.

The best way to not miss out on news of my releases and back list is by subscribing to my newsletter at ***www. stellaquinnauthor.com/subscribe***

Happy reading (and escape!)

Stella Quinn xxx

# CHAPTER 1

"Tell me again," muttered Katie through the gray furry muzzle of the smelliest costume she had ever worn, "why *I* have to be the one to dress up as the dog?"

Her friend Ramon jangled the fundraising bucket he was holding towards a loved-up couple sharing a giant stick of candy floss. "I gave you a choice, fundraising or marketing. You chose marketing."

She didn't know whether to laugh or howl. "Huh. If I'd known you were tricking me with fancy words, I'd have paid more attention."

"Look," said Ramon, nudging her with his shoulder. "There's a photographer coming from the local paper. Now's our chance."

She couldn't see very clearly through the eye-slits cut into the dense fur of her fake head. Food stalls and tourists filled the grassy park and the beach full of market stalls was a dizzy blur of color. "Where?"

"Near the jazz quartet on the wharf. Let's get over there

and play for the camera. Who knows, we may get the front page of the *Cove to Coast Herald*."

Katie felt her stomach sink like she'd just dropped off the top of one of those beach-side rollercoaster rides. Why, oh why, had she agreed to accompany Ramon to the Summer Festival fundraiser? She was so much happier home on her sofa, binge-watching cooking shows with her dog—her real dog—snoozing at her feet. "When you say *play*," she said, "you better not mean you're going to throw me a frisbee."

Ramon's chuckle was rich enough to win a ribbon at the fudge stall. "Relax, Katie. I know you hate being sociable. I'll hold the bucket and talk up the feel-good benefits of donating to the refuge, and you can hold the sign and look...um...like a good dog."

Huh. People thought she hated being sociable? She scrabbled around in the corner of the Gold Coast Dog Refuge stall until she had their donations sign gripped in her oversized furry paws, then turned in the direction of the wharf. "Let's do this," she said. She could worry about why Ramon's comment had stung later.

Navigating the crowd wouldn't have been easy for a wiry pickpocket. It was certainly not easy for a grown woman in a great furry suit with poorly cut eyeholes. Their trek to the wharf was slowed by all the festival goers who were keen to donate to their cause.

"We find homes for abandoned dogs," Ramon told a young woman who ran up to pop a twenty in the bucket.

"Yes, all our dogs are vaccinated, neutered, and put through behavioral training," he said in answer to another query.

Katie stumbled over an abandoned tent peg wedged in the

grass and found herself jerked backwards as someone hauled on her tail. "Excuse me," she said, swinging around to face a toddler with a sticky face and a ten-dollar bill clasped in his chubby hand.

"For the lonely dog-dogs," he said.

"Um…woof," she said. Man, she had so not thought this through. Should she speak and destroy this kid's belief in giant magic dogs who walked on two legs and collected donations at parks? Or was woofing an appropriate way of saying thank you to a sugar-fueled toddler with a big heart?

"Nearly there," said Ramon in her ear, and he thanked the toddler, popped the proffered bill into his bucket, and steered her around until she was again facing the wharf. He kept his hand under her arm until he'd schmoozed his way in front of the photographer like the public relations expert he was. "Need a photo of us, pal?" he said brightly. "Festivals and fundraising make a terrific headline."

"Sure," the man said. "Can't promise you'll make the paper, but happy to take one. I'll need your names for the disclaimer."

"Ramon Bowtell," said Ramon. "And this is Ka—"

"This is Buddy the Dog," she said firmly. "Buddy is the mascot for the Gold Coast Pet Refuge. He's very photogenic."

The photographer grinned. "Ramon and Buddy," he said, keying a note into his phone. "Hold the bucket and sign a little higher and say cheese."

Katie obliged by holding the sign up, then turned to Ramon when the photographer moved away. "How are we doing for donations? I'm getting a little hot in here."

Ramon gave the bucket a jangle. "Feels heavier than it did

three hours ago. Why don't we keep walking through the crowds for another half hour, then call it a day."

Half a minute would have been enough for her, but after Ramon's comment about her social habits, it seemed too awkward to say so. Finally, though, she was waving Ramon and his full bucket goodbye and slipping to the edge of the crowd.

If only she could remember where she'd parked her car.

The alley behind the bakery? She poked her head around the corner of the old canning factory that had been converted into an artisan brewery. Nope, not up that alley. Must be the next.

Sweat trickled down between her shoulder blades as she hurried her steps. Fresh air and at least a liter of water to drink, that's what she needed. She was dehydrated, that's why she'd taken Ramon's comment to heart. Dehydrated, not unsociable.

Hauling her keys out of the hidden pocket behind the fur of the dog belly, she rounded the next corner just as a flash of color popped into her narrow field of vision.

"Oof," she said, as a broad chest in a snug-fitting running shirt knocked her off her feet.

"Oh no!" said a deep voice. "I'm so sorry. I didn't see you."

She looked up, but all she could see was the inner webbing of the dog head. She grabbed the snout and twisted it around until the eye-slits were aligned again. A man stood over her, tall and fit in exercise gear and a baseball cap, his chest heaving as though he'd been running for some time.

"I'm fine," she said. "Sorry, I can't see so well in this outfit."

The top half of his face was shadowed by his cap, but she

could see his lips twitch. "Gotta say, I've never run into a five-foot dog before. You need a hand getting up?"

She held out a paw, and the guy hauled her to her feet.

"Thanks," she said.

"Going to the festival?"

"Just leaving. There's only so much fun a dog can take in one afternoon. How about you?"

He looked over her shoulder to where the music and tourists were in full swing across the esplanade and foreshore. "Yeah, crowds aren't really my thing. I'm just running past. You sure you're okay?"

"I'm fine, thanks. But—"

She'd just noticed a streak of red on his jawline. She gestured to it with a furry foreleg. "You might have grazed yourself. There's a little, um, mark there."

He swiped his hand over his face and winced. "Smacked my head into the bricks coming round the corner. It's fine."

"There's a first aid station set up by the wharf."

His face, the part she could see of it, slid from friendly to sad. "Seriously, it's fine. I like to save my panic moments for the big stuff these days."

Oh, wow, had she touched a nerve? She should say something, but what?

"Well," he said. "I'd better, er…"

"Keep going. Sure. Me too."

She watched through her fuzzy eye-slits as the man with the sad face slipped through the crowd, then disappeared onto the cliff walk.

It was a view she was used to. People left her. That's just the way it was.

# CHAPTER 2

"I think I'm cured," Anton Price said to his therapist, first thing Monday morning.

Dr. Alice Goodly raised her eyebrows. "Really? You don't call me for months, then show up without an appointment to tell me you're all better now."

He smiled. "Okay, it sounded a lot more reasonable when I was practicing it in my car on the way over here."

Alice Goodly must have trained her eyebrows as psychotherapy consultants, because a lot of the time, she just sat there while they did all the work. This was one of those times…silence, just those disbelieving eyebrows daring him to speak.

He broke first. "I ran through a festival last weekend. Hundreds of people, noise, photographers—I didn't even flinch."

"Did they know who you were?"

"No, but—"

"Were they at a book signing? At a book launch? At a publicity event?"

"No, but—"

"I see."

He tried to speak up, but those eyebrows were doing their thing again. Alice drummed her fingers on the desk.

"You still running?"

"Every day."

The left eyebrow frowned. "Like—*every* day? Obsessively, or just because you enjoy it?"

He tried not to smile. "Not obsessively, Doctor. I have not replaced panic attacks with obsessive running."

"Good to hear. How's the cooking coming along?"

"I could open a restaurant."

"Really?" She made a note on the open file in front of her.

"What did you write down?"

Her brown eyes met his. "You really want to know?"

"I really do."

"I wrote 'ego unimpaired.'"

"Huh."

She grinned then, and he knew he was forgiven for missing the last half dozen appointments.

"Seriously, Alice. I really do feel like I've mastered my panic reaction."

"I want to believe you, Anton, I really do, but when you don't visit, it limits my ability to be useful."

"I'm sorry."

"Tell me what's been working for you."

He leaned back in one of the faux-leather chairs that Alice had decorated her rooms with. "Working at the paper, mostly. It's routine, it gets me out of my house…it's peaceful. I think peace has restored me."

It was the right eyebrow's turn to question his words. "*Too peaceful, I think.*"

"What do you mean?"

"Julia still embroidering you those cute little self-help samplers?"

He should never have let that slip to Alice; she'd be taunting him with it forever. "She's a grandmother, Alice. Embroidery is what grandmothers do."

Alice neatened the folder on her desk until it sat exactly flush with the edge. "You're feeling restored, calm, as though you can cope, but you're not testing yourself, Anton. You're working one day a week in an office where they treat you like their treasured pet. Have you been to New York lately? Done a television interview? Answered your mail?"

She had him there.

"You see? You want to know if you really are over your anxiety? You need to test yourself."

"How?"

"Start small. The next time an opportunity comes your way—an invitation, an offer of work—ask yourself if the idea of accepting it makes you feel uncomfortable."

He had a bad feeling about where this was going. "And then?"

She shut his folder with a snap. "Then you accept it. Get out of your peaceful little rut, Anton. Get uncomfortable, cope with something new and unexpected, then come back here and tell me you're cured."

Something new and unexpected. Where was he going to find *that* in Redwood Cove?

# CHAPTER 3

*K*atie pulled the industrial-gray earphones from her head and turned to her supervisor. "Sign me out, Andy. I'm at my time limit for the week."

"Again? I thought you were taking *less* shifts this summer, not more."

She picked up her cup and took a swig, then grimaced. Eesh. Somewhere between the light plane coming in at the wrong angle and the helicopter pilot who must have found his commercial license in the bottom of a cereal box, her coffee had grown as tepid as...well, as her heart.

No. She was not going to live her life being defined by the cheap shots her ex had thrown at her before he packed up his apartment and took off for Someplace Else, U.S.A. She forced herself to take another sip. Her coffee was as tepid as a mudpuddle, she thought. There, see? Her similes had moved on, and so had she. Go her.

Her boss, Andy, was standing, hands on hips, surveying the busy row of uniformed staff manning the controls below the huge window. "Who's working the second airstrip now that you've clocked out?"

She sat her cup back on the desk and started paying attention. Air traffic controllers weren't paid to be distracted at work. "Fabiana. We've done the handover. She's got a commercial plane due in twenty minutes, the noon commuter from San Francisco, then nothing until two p.m. unless we get a take-off request from a local pilot."

Andy looked at Fabiana, who was already snapping instructions into her mouthpiece, then typed a few notes into the tablet that he was never without. "Great. See you on Monday?"

"I've got a day off on Monday. I'm the Tuesday afternoon shift next week."

"Gotcha. Enjoy your weekend."

She picked her coat up from the back of her chair and checked her watch. Rats, she was behind schedule. She'd been hoping to spend a moment or two alone on the outdoor observation deck of the control tower before leaving. Her safe place, she thought of it...above the world, rolling fields and ocean spread below her, and the deep rugged green of Griffin State Park looming behind. No people, no pain, just her and the view.

Maybe she could still sneak in a few seconds? She edged away from Andy, hoping to make a getaway. Her boss was an angel, but he was a chatty angel, and she was on a timetable this afternoon. "Bye Andy."

"And when I say *enjoy*," he said, settling his hip on a desk as though he was about to give her a monologue on how she ought to spend her weekend, "I don't mean wallowing in your kitchen baking cookies, Katie."

She smiled at him. "No baking, I promise." She checked her watch again. She was out of time for view-gazing if she was going to get a full training session in at the refuge. Her quiet time on the observatory deck would have to wait.

She set off for the elevator that would drop her a hundred feet to the bottom of Redwood Cove Airport's control tower.

"I mean dancing!" Andy called after her. "Having a reckless white wine spritzer at a café overlooking the water! Meeting some new guy already!"

She gave her boss a wave as the elevator doors closed and shut him out. After working in the refuge's fundraising stall at the Summer Festival last weekend, she was looking forward to a quiet weekend at home. Andy meant well but being happily married himself for near-on forty years made him something of an optimist when it came to matters of the human heart.

Katie rested her head against the cold steel of the elevator wall. Optimism was a quality she'd learned to live without.

# CHAPTER 4

*A*nton balanced his takeout coffee on his laptop case as he opened the door to the local newspaper office. The *Cove to Coast Herald* occupied the ground floor of a historic, red-brick building, and dust motes spun as sunlight came through the door with him into the dim interior.

"You there, Danny? Jules?"

A thud from the back room preceded a mop of gray hair above grass-green reading glasses popping around the inner doorframe. "Anton. Just the person we need. Bring your handsome manly arms this way, would you, pet? We've got a crisis unfolding back here."

Just the word *crisis* was enough to get his heartbeat accelerating into an unsteady canter. He took a breath. For a guy who used to make a living off crises and disasters, he should be better at coping by now. "You're joking, right, Jules?"

"Sorry, pet, I should have chosen my words better. Just a minor kerfuffle is all…we've locked ourselves out of the safe. Wait, is that a cut on your face, Anton Price?"

"It's nothing, just a scratch. A brick leapt out at me when I was running last Sunday, and I keep nicking it with my razor. Tell me about the safe."

"Oh, well, it's not too keen to open this morning. Danny's sure the combination's written in one of his old diaries, but we're too short to reach the archive boxes."

Anton set his gear down on the desk he used on his weekly excursions to the newspaper office, then headed into the storage room after Julie. An office chair on caster wheels was wedged up against the bank of ancient mahogany box shelves lining the room. Atop the chair was the three-legged stool that was normally tucked into the utility kitchen, and atop that, flailing his arms like a wind turbine, was Danny Pargeter, proprietor and editor of Redwood Cove's oldest independent newspaper.

"What in heck are you doing up there, Danny? Step down already; didn't you turn seventy-five just last month?"

"Don't sass me, young feller. There's folks running for president of this country that are older than me; no one's telling them to step down."

Anton grinned. "We can save political debates for another day, Danny. Here, let me help you get down." He took a grip on the old man's arm and helped him make his way back to the floor.

"Got a few years in me yet, Anton, my boy."

"More than a few unless you break your neck doing circus tricks back here."

Julie giggled behind him. "I wanted to say that, but I was afraid he'd sack me."

"Still might," grumbled Danny.

Anton winked at Julie. They both knew Danny would do no such thing. Julie was as much a part of the office as Danny and the dust motes and the ancient *Cove to Coast Herald* sign hanging above the front door of the building.

He pulled the stool off the chair and made a mental note to toss it in the dumpster on his way home. Offices which employed senior citizens had no business keeping death traps on the premises. "Okay. What are we looking for? An old diary?"

He pulled the office chair out of the way and tested the strength of the shelves. Solid as the hundred-year-old mahogany trees they were made from. He climbed up a couple and peered into the upper reaches of the cupboard. Dust as thick as felt covered the surface, an ancient typewriter that a collector would give away their firstborn to acquire, and stacks—literally, stacks—of diaries. Black marker decorated the spines with dates: 2019, 2016...1997...he looked across the row and found 1982, 1967...was that *1956*?

"I wrote the combination in the front page the year I got the safe, isn't that right, Julie?"

"Yes, pet. So as we'd have it safe."

Anton hung from the shelving. "Any clues as to what year that was? You've got more diaries up here than the local library has books, Danny. I can't believe you've kept them all."

Danny's chest puffed out like a bantam's. "For my memoirs."

"Really?" He chuckled. Danny was such an old sweetheart; Anton couldn't imagine his memoirs having any of the drama and scandal modern memoirs seemed to require.

"I've got stories you wouldn't believe, son."

Anton's smile faded. He would have loved to have heard those stories once...maybe even have used them for inspiration for one of his thriller novels.

Not anymore. The day the world's news headlines started resembling the plot of one of his bestselling books was the day stories died. For him, anyway.

He felt his biceps starting to burn. "Give me a hint which decade you think it was, and I can start passing some of these down."

Danny and Julie conferred below him. "The nineties," said Julie.

"As recently as that?" said Danny.

"The nineties weren't recent," said Anton. "The twenty-twenties won't be recent soon, either, if you don't decide real quick. Come on, even my handsome manly arms can't keep me perched here forever."

"Youngsters today," grumbled Danny. "So impatient."

He grinned. "I'm not that young." Long past the big three-zero, but four-zero wasn't quite around the corner...but who was counting? Years didn't matter anymore, the same way deadlines didn't and writing books didn't. "Okay, I'm passing down the diaries from the nineties, then I'm climbing down. I'll bring a ladder from home if we need to get the rest of these, okay?"

"Pass 'em down, son."

He pulled a few books out of the stack, feeling the decades-old dust tickle his nose, and dropped them down.

"Any luck?" he said to Danny and Julie, who spread them open across the table and engrossed themselves in the entries.

They muttered something unintelligible, so he decided to listen to his shrieking biceps and climb down. "Let me know if you want me to bring my ladder. I'm heading out front to typeset next week's *Page Seventeen* into the digital file."

"Oh, look there," Julie was saying, snuggled into Danny's

shoulder. "May 1996. We did the feature on that juvenile humpback whale who beached himself, and all the residents helped push him out to sea."

Anton contemplated looking over their shoulders and joining them on their trip down memory lane, but hesitated. He had the crossword to set and his other columns to finish. Memory lane could wait.

"Here's an old one," he heard Danny murmur. "Look at that picture...has to be a young Carol Graves. This'll be the story we ran when she nearly drowned. That was an issue to remember."

"Saved by a dog," Julia said.

He made his way back out front to his desk, opened his laptop, and logged into the design software. A dog hadn't been around when he'd needed saving from panic attacks, but crosswords had. And peace and quiet, and his therapist. He only hoped that had been enough. He took a swig from his coffee and grimaced. Eesh. He'd spent so long swinging from the shelves in the back room that it had grown cold.

No matter. He could microwave it later. It wasn't as though he had anything else to do.

# CHAPTER 5

*K*atie glanced at her watch as she pulled into the timber cottage she and her sister had grown up in. She had time for a quick change into her training gear, and then she would be on her way.

Geraniums bloomed on either side of the gravel drive, so red they ought to be little pots of cheerfulness, but all they did was remind her how much she missed her uncle.

*His* geraniums bloomed, *his* whimsical wind chime swung from the redwood by the gate, made from shells and driftwood he'd collected from the nearby beach.

She sighed. A year he'd been gone, and she still thought of the house as his.

A deep woof reached her ears as she opened the door of her rusty old hatchback. Okay, *that* was not Uncle Roly's. He had been strictly a cat guy.

"Rosie girl," she called.

She didn't have long to wait. The massive retriever galloped around the corner of the house from the back yard where she liked to spend her alone time digging this-is-what-happens-when-you-leave-me holes beneath the hibiscus hedge.

"There's my favorite friend ever," Katie said, as Rose cleared the low front fence in a graceful leap. She'd tried to train her out of leaping fences in a single bound, she really had, but Rosie *loved* jumping. If she'd had longer legs and a mane, Katie could have entered her in the local pony show jumping competition.

Besides, Rose only ever jumped the front fence to welcome her home, and she didn't have the heart to deny herself the little rush of being so, so welcomed. At least Rose's other habits weren't so problematic: collecting the letters from the mailbox and taking Katie's socks out of her sneakers and lining them up like pastel snails in front of the washing machine. Rose loved helping almost as much as she loved jumping.

Katie took a step back as Rosie thrust her long golden muzzle into the pocket of her Redwood Cove Airport jacket. "Sorry, Rose Petal, there's no liver treats in there. But give me ten minutes to change, and we'll go on an adventure, all right?"

Rosie scampered about her like a spring lamb, so she had to assume that, yes, anything she suggested would be totally all right.

Rosie was that kind of a dog: chill, enthusiastic, and always ready to go.

Which was why, Katie thought as Rose pulled the mail from the letterbox and followed her up the wide plank steps onto the porch, she made the perfect therapy dog for the inmates of Heartbreak Row at the Gold Coast Dog Refuge.

She pushed her key into the lock and opened the door,

standing back so Rosie could rocket in ahead of her. The ghost of sixty years of Uncle Roly's cat ownership must linger in some way obvious only to dogs, because, as always, Rosie dumped the mail on the sofa and then gave the polished floorboards and colorful rugs a thorough sniff.

She sifted through the envelopes while Rose finished her cat patrol. Utilities bill, ugh, that could be opened later. Ditto for the property taxes. Who knew inheriting half a house could prove to be so expensive? She flipped through to the final envelope in her hands and smiled.

Aha. The one she'd been waiting for, pale blue with a messy scrawl looping through her name and address on the front. Her sister worked as a loans officer for SantaCal Bank, but in her spare time—because, hey, over-achiever—Veronica flipped houses for a living. Her weekends were usually spent ripping out drywall or painting newel posts, which left little time for driving ninety minutes to visit her sister in Redwood Cove.

The letters were Vee's way of staying connected, and, because Vee was Vee, she liked to turn them into a competition. School sports? Veronica was always on the A team, Katie on the B team. Charades at Thanksgiving? Veronica was entertaining the crowd with a flawless mime of every character in Shrek, while Katie was still deciding how many fingers she needed to wave in the air for her two-syllable movie title.

A decade and a half later, crosswords were the latest form of competitive torture Vee had chosen to inflict on her, a game about as much fun as thumbscrews for the laterally challenged, as Katie was. Where Vee was all impulse and creativity, Katie was the sensible one. The one who relied on routine and logic.

She looked down at Rosie before cracking the seal on the envelope. "I suck at games."

Rosie woofed agreeably.

"Thanks for the support, my sweet."

Katie pulled the letter from the envelope and the ripped-out *Page Seventeen* from the local paper that her sister expected her to entertain herself with. Ha! The puzzle page? She had no interest in that at all, but the weekly old-school letter from Vee, filled with gossip and chitchat? That, she loved.

She dropped the newspaper page to the counter along with the other junk mail and scanned the letter.

*Hey there, sis! Here's your* Page Seventeen *for the week. This week's clue is a tricky anagram. You'll crack this one, I know you will. Five across...you know what to do!*

Hmm. Optimistic thinking, but still. Maybe this week she *would* crack it.

She looked at the grid of black and white newsprint. "Let's see, five across," she muttered, scanning the list of clues next to the crossword box. Aha.

"Listen to this, Rosie. Five across, eight letters: *Bring flowers to the migraine sufferer? Almost.* That mean anything at all to you?"

Rosie was standing by the coat stand at the front door where her lead and harness were dangling from an ornate brass hook. Her expression clearly indicated she had no such time for tomfoolery, let's get outside already.

Katie grinned at her dog. "Saved me again, Rose. Great idea, we can torture ourselves later. Let's get going."

She tossed her sister's letter and newspaper page onto the counter with her airport I.D. lanyard. She had all evening to read it...all weekend, even...because there was no chance she was following Andy's advice and heading out for some hipster spritzer and opening herself up to another bout of heartbreak. No chance at all.

THE ROAD out to the refuge where she and Rosie volunteered each week led away from the coast. As the tidy houses and prettily hedged sidewalks of Redwood Cove thinned behind them, the industrial precinct took over. Cinder block warehouses towered over dusty lots filled with long-haul trucks and busy workers on forklifts. The animal refuge ran on a budget so small, it was struggling to find a decent place to operate from.

For months now, it had been tucked into the back of a distribution warehouse for Dorma Valley Winery, who had loaned them the space for free. These poor pups didn't have prairie grass to roll on or sea breeze to move through their fur.

They were living on borrowed time, and even the hard work of the refuge volunteers couldn't quite snuff out the air of desperation.

And nowhere at the refuge was quite as desperate as the row of kennels set within a double fence line of six-foot chain mesh. Heartbreak Row, Katie called it. And that was where she and Rosie were headed.

Ramon waved her in through the gate, and she marveled again at how lucky the refuge was to have him on the team.

He might look like he'd given up a career in pro-wrestling to become a volunteer, but he was a public relations dynamo who had done wonders for the refuge out of the old trailer they used as headquarters.

"Wassup, Katie?" he said. "Rose, my girl, high five."

Rosie sat up in the passenger seat of Katie's hatchback as high as her travel harness would allow. High five was a trick she'd mastered as a pup, and it never failed to extract a liver treat from Ramon.

"We're working with Prince again today, Ramon."

"No problem. You need me to come give you a hand, hit the alarm button, same as always."

"Will do."

She let out the clutch, and her ancient muffler belched as she took off through the cement and kennel maze to the visitor's parking lot. Ramon spent a lot of time out here, way more than her. She wondered if his friends called him unsociable, too.

Parking, she let Rose out of the car and headed deeper into the refuge grounds. Prince was a two-year-old spaniel-Labrador cross who had been abandoned by his owners. After a re-homing trial that had ended in an elderly lady being dragged off her feet when he lunged on the lead to attack another dog, Prince had been brought to the refuge and housed in the row of isolation kennels they used for the dogs suffering from fear aggression.

That's where Katie and Rose came in. If they could socialize Prince to overcome his instinctual *fight* response, he'd have a future. If they failed?

Katie blew out a breath. She didn't like to think about what happened on the rare times they failed. Some dogs were beyond her skill set to train. Even cute-as-pie fluffy black heartbreakers like Prince.

Before they reached Heartbreak Row, she unclipped Rose's lead and tucked it into her backpack. Rose always did as she was told in training sessions, and Prince didn't respond well to leads. "Time for work, Rose," she said to her dog, who knew the difference between being on-duty and off.

On-duty meant being calm, and still, and waiting for hand signals.

Off-duty meant leaping over front fences and digging fun holes in Uncle Roly's back garden.

Prince started barking like a maniac and throwing himself at the gate of his kennel as soon he set eyes on Rose, which was his standard response to any four-legged threat.

"Hey, there, buddy," she said, in the calm, low voice she used for dog training.

Prince took his eyes off Rose for a second, long enough to accept a liver treat from her hand and be rewarded for being a good boy, then his hackles were back up and he was barking again.

"We're here to do some work, Prince. It'll be fun, just wait and see."

She turned to Rose and directed her to enter the large training enclosure, where they could work with Prince without worrying about other dogs coming in or Prince getting out. She waited until Rose had assumed her position at the far end of the yard, then she slipped into Prince's kennel and clipped his lead to his collar.

"Okay, Prince," she said.

He was happy to see her, of that there was no doubt. He loved being petted, and he sniffed her knees and hands and wagged his tail. She led him into the training yard, and the second he laid eyes on Rose, the frantic barking started up again, accompanied by him throwing himself about at the end of his lead like a marlin on the end of a fishing line.

"I know, buddy. But we're going to walk past her and around her again and again and again until you've worked out she's not a threat."

She clicked at him under her tongue and began walking at a fast clip around the yard. Every time he looked up at her, she slipped him a liver treat, every time he was quiet, she slipped him a liver treat…and finally, after a dozen laps or more, his frantic tugging settled down and his eyes stopped rolling in his head.

She gave his ears a quick rub. "Not calm, are you, Prince? But calm*er*. And that's a win. You ready to get a little closer?"

She gave Rose a hand signal, and Rose stood up, walked forward a couple of feet, then sat smartly back down again. Prince growled, low in his throat, but he remained still.

"Progress," she muttered.

She worked with the dogs for an hour, and by the time she'd finished, the sun was slanting low shadows through the chain mesh fence.

Ramon had wandered over from the office and was leaning up against her car.

"He's responding well," he said.

"Yes, I thought so. I might work him a couple more times with Rosie, then take him on a walk in a public space."

"You're a great asset to the refuge, Katie. We're lucky to have you."

She punched him in the arm. "Back at you, Ramon. These dogs need us all."

"Pity we can't get the donations up."

"You telling me I wasn't a hit in my dog suit?"

He grinned. "The festival stall brought in lots of donations, which will pay for dog food and vet bills. But we need to think big, Katie. I'd love to move us out of this industrial park and find us some actual grass. Trees for the dogs to pee on, instead of cement walls."

"I know. Still, this place is rent free. It was good of the winery to let us use this space."

Ramon gave a nod in the direction of the main gate. "I'm heading out soon; the night watchman is here. You ready to go?"

"Sure. Sorry, we ran a little overtime today. I'm sorry I can't get here earlier, but my shifts at work have been kind of crazy lately."

Ramon pulled her in for a hug. "You come when you can, Katie girl. I'll see you soon, hey?"

"You bet."

Katie secured Rose in the car, then slid in behind the wheel and hit the road for home. Full-time traffic controller, part-time therapy dog volunteer...*that's* why she didn't have time for socially awkward spritzers down on the waterfront.

She was busy, darn it. Not unsociable.

# CHAPTER 6

*A*nton usually ran his four-mile track along the cliff walk at dawn, but *Page Seventeen* had kept him busy all day, so it was late afternoon by the time he was ready to hunt down his sneakers.

The crossword was never the problem, it was the agony aunt letters that had him tearing his hair out each week. He'd have ditched that column like a shot if Danny hadn't put the emotional thumbscrews on him. According to Danny, the residents of Redwood Cove would fall into a decline if they didn't have a personal letters column to read each week.

At least he, or Anna Tugoy as he called himself for that part of his page, had a psychology degree in his dim, distant past. As little as he relished dishing out bland answers to zany questions, at least he could dish them out with the mantra of "do no harm".

He grinned, thinking how thoroughly his three sisters would roast him if they caught wind of the fact that he was masquerading in a local newspaper as an agony aunt. Being the youngest, he was treated by all three of his sisters as though he was barely competent to use a toaster or change the diaper of one of their growing broods of kids. They'd laugh even more at the thought of all the letters he received addressed to *Dear Anna*.

He treated his fake persona like she was a character in one of the books he used to write. In his head, Anna was a mid-fifties spinster with kooky glasses and a head of curls that she regularly dyed a loud, fire-engine red. She ate Tootsie Rolls for breakfast, drank tea by the gallon, and had a regrettable habit of asking her nephews for a selfie when she saw them at Thanksgiving.

He stopped in town near the end of his run to clear his postal box. Should have bought a bag, he thought, as the dozens of letters threatened to scatter from his hands all over the street.

He nodded hello to the café owners, who were busy setting up tables and umbrellas for the weekend cocktail crowd.

It would make a good photo. He pulled his phone out of his running shorts and lined up a row of umbrellas, green and red and orange, blooming along the esplanade like giant flowers. Maybe he could upload it to the paper's Reel Life account and choose his own Happy Snap for once. *Photo by Anton: This photo of the Redwood Cove beach makes me happy because...* He frowned. That was the problem, wasn't it? Was he, Anton Price, happy?

He'd kind of forgotten what happy felt like, which was probably why he had a slightly unhealthy obsession with sticking other people's happy photographs in his newspaper column. Sometimes he even scoped out where the photo had been taken and stood there, trying to understand why a place, a view, could inspire happiness in others.

"Ant, long time no see."

He turned at the voice. "Dash, hey. Good to see you." You couldn't live in Redwood Cove and not know Dash. Part television celebrity, part hometown hero, he was also one of the few friends Anton kept in touch with.

"You still hiding out in that cottage of yours?"

He held up the bundle of letters in his hand. "Keeping myself busy."

Dash nodded. "Well, that busy ever translates into a new book, let me know. We'd love to have you on Good Morning Gold Coast."

He grinned. "Nice try, buddy."

Dash had been trying to get him on that show for years.

"Seriously, man. We never see you. You can't stay glued to your keyboard forever; get the next book finished already."

It was easier to smile and nod and mutter something about writer's block than admit he'd lost his mojo. "It's a slow process."

"Too bad. I love those books."

Yeah. He had too, once.

"Got time for a beer?"

"Next time, Dash," he promised. He waggled the thick stack of letters. "Better get stuck into this."

"Fan mail?"

He laughed. "Maybe. Bound to see some bills in there, too."

"Ain't that always the way," said his friend, waving him goodbye.

Anton's thoughts spun back to photography as he made his way up the hill. The idea for his *Happy Snaps* column had come to him when he'd been filling in a long, blank evening scrolling through other people's social media posts. People—

meh, he scrolled on by. Pets, memes, politics, news stories—he scrolled past them all.

The landscape shots always caught his attention, though. Beach scenes taken here in town, or wilder shots from further along the coast where the Pacific Ocean rolled into steep granite cliffs. Rolling prairies of wildflowers, surgically neat rows of manicured grape vines, the charm of a historic building front framed by maple leaves in the full fire of autumn.

He found them…soothing. And, boy howdy, was he in a mood to be soothed. His headspace had—he could admit it—gone haywire when his latest book's plot suddenly seemed to be a script the real world was trapped in.

The *Happy Snaps* column on *Page Seventeen* of the *Cove to Coast Herald* was the way he'd found to move forward. Readers shared a photo to the newspaper's Reel Life page, along with a few paragraphs on why that place was important to them and how being there made them feel better. He'd kickstarted the column with a few of his own photos, taken from the walled garden of the restored lighthouse-keeper's cottage that he'd bought back when his books were selling like hotcakes in every airport in the nation. The sun setting across the bay, the gilded fluke of a whale caught by sunlight as seawater streamed across it.

He hadn't had to use his own photos for long, because the column went viral, at least in their town. Turned out, he wasn't the only one who loved scenic views.

On his usual dawn runs, he might find himself staring at a bleached log in the corner of a rocky cove and think: *Ah! Photo by Amanda: she sat here after her father's funeral and remembered how he taught her to swim.* Or he'd be walking through the older district in town, where the shop fronts were painted in pastel colors and tourists ate ice-cream and exclaimed over the pretty park by the grassy area before the beach, and he'd see an old clock perched in the high brick tower of a municipal building and think: *Photo by Peter: married his girl here before she went to the war in Iraq. She's been home a long time now, but she's suffered, and they like to come here to feel good and have a take-out coffee on the sand and think about what foolish kids they'd once been.*

He reached the narrow wooden gate set deep within the stone wall that circled his garden and let himself in.

A beer. A shower. But first, duty. This wad of letters wasn't fan mail for Anton Price, thriller writer. His agent dealt with that, and since he hadn't been answering his agent's calls for months, who knew what was waiting for him—fan mail or hate mail, he wasn't interested.

The only letters he got these days were for his new vocation: *Page Seventeen* in the *Cove to Coast Herald.*

He flipped through the mail. Ones addressed to Anna Tugoy he could go through later when his laptop was handy and he was in a mood to read a heap of half-foolish, half-sweet requests like, "Dear Anna, my best friend never offers to buy me lunch even though I buy her lunch every week." A couple for his crossword column; excellent. There were some keen crossword enthusiasts out there in the community who sent him clues they'd invented. He always used them when he could. A buff envelope with the tell-tale logo of his publisher on the front stopped him cold.

He should read it.

He *really* should read it.

He took a long breath in, then pushed it out just as slowly.

Majoring in psychology at college had only ever landed him one job. He'd barely completed the minimum hours to receive his practicing license when his first book was picked up by a publisher and took off like a freight train.

But some lessons stayed learned, like how to calm himself the heck down.

He looked at the envelope for a long, long time. They'd just want him to finish the last manuscript he was working on, another five-hundred-page megabook of guns and bombs and villainous one-eyed assassins.

No, nope, never. He chucked the letter into the trash and headed inside to boot up the shower. He was a chicken, yes. But he was a chicken who had a newspaper page to write, so he'd better get clucking.

# CHAPTER 7

*K*atie remembered the letter waiting for her when she was midway through slicing up a jalapeno chile to toss in the wok with her greens. She flicked the gas off on the stove, perched on the stool at the kitchen counter, and pulled everything from the envelope.

The crossword clue could wait...it wasn't as though she ever worked them out anyway. She opened the folded letter and started galloping through it, a smile on her face. Sure, she could call Veronica any day of the week, but this letter gig they had running was *fun*.

*Hey there, sis! Grab Page Seventeen. This week's clue is a tricky anagram. You'll crack this one, I know you will. Five across...you know what to do!*

*How's work? How's the house? How's Rose?*

*Anyhoo, enough about you, because drumroll: I have NEWS.*

*I have to make a confession first. You know how I told you I moved up to Maple Ridge because of a promotion? Well, that was only partly true. I moved because I had a crush on this guy at work down there in Redwood Cove and I made a fool of myself at an office party. There was a job going at this branch of the bank, so I applied for it.*

*I'm sorry I didn't tell you when this was all happening, but I was too embarrassed.*

*But...fast forward eight months and boom! How quickly things can change.*

*I've met someone. THE someone. I'm feeling so, so good about this, Katie. Like, the luckiest girl in the world. And to think it was Tuna Yango who helped me out, LOL!!! Gotta love the irony of getting personal life hacks from a crossword compiler!*

*Call me for the details too juicy to put in print. (\*waggles eyebrows up and down).*

*Vee xx*

Katie dropped the letter like it was a hotcake and grabbed for her phone. Veronica had been seeing a guy and had kept the news a secret? It boggled the mind. Vee was the chattiest person in the state of California.

She hit speed dial and waited for her sister to pick up. And waited...and waited. The phone rang out and switched over to a recorded message. She waited for her sister's voice to stop, then spoke into the phone. "Vee, it's me. Call me anytime. No hour is too late to share juicy details with your sister. Later."

Hmm. She ran her eyes over the page again. Tuna Yango... what on earth? Sounded like a food dish or a South American dance craze. It also sounded weirdly familiar.

She flicked the gas back on under her wilting stir fry and carried on cooking dinner. Vee would call any minute now and explain all.

VEE DIDN'T CALL. Not that night, not the next day, not any time during the week.

By Thursday, Katie felt mildly anxious. Friday, she had the day off, so she and Rose spent the morning at the refuge working with Prince. After lunch, she ripped weeds out of Uncle Roly's flower beds and thought dark thoughts about selfish sisters who left their relatives wondering why they couldn't return a simple phone call.

When her weekly letter wasn't in the bunch of mail Rose collected from the mailbox and dumped onto the sofa, her mild anxiety ratcheted into full-blown alarm. At four p.m. she stopped kidding herself that she was okay and called the Maple Ridge branch of SantaCal Bank, only to learn that her sister had called in to take some personal leave last Thursday and hadn't been heard from since.

If she'd had a blood pressure machine, she would have strapped it to her arm and taken hers, because she was so not okay with her sister going missing like this. Personal leave? What on earth for? If she was sick, she'd be in the apartment she rented in the historic quarter of Maple Ridge, so why hadn't she returned Katie's calls?

She'd have to drive up there, and she'd have to do it now. Her shift in the tower started at ten a.m. next day, and Maple Ridge was a three-hour round trip along the coast then up into the Santa Cruz Mountains.

"Road trip, Rosie?"

The dog pushed her heavy head onto Katie's thigh and gave a soft whuffle.

"Atta girl."

She was an hour into the drive up over the mountain pass into Santa Cruz County when she remembered what—or, to be more precise, who—Tuna Yango was. She (or he?) was the compiler of the cryptic crossword Veronica sent her each week. The one she usually ignored.

# CHAPTER 8

The brass bell tied to the door of the *Cove to Coast Herald* offices tinkled, but Anton ignored it. Jules was around somewhere. Or Danny. The two of them loved nothing more than spending the morning chattering over the front counter to some Redwood Cove octogenarian who wanted to put an advertisement in the paper or talk about their new whizz-bang golf-cart.

*Can't keep up in sport?* he typed into the software program that typeset his page. *Help is available.* Not the cleverest clue he'd ever dreamed up, but he liked to keep enough easy clues in each week to help the beginners crack the harder ones.

The bell on the counter was the next one to ding, and he sighed, hit save on his laptop, and peered around the filing cabinet and drooping fern to see who was needing attention.

"Jules?" he called. "Someone out front to see you."

He waited, but the usual click-clack of Julie's needle-thin heels was notably absent. He blew out a breath. Looked like he could add office receptionist to his list of alternate careers now that thriller writing had been kicked to the curb.

He rose to his feet. "Sorry, no one seems to be around—"

Oh. The second his gaze locked onto the woman standing at the front counter with a massive, shaggy golden dog at her side, his ability to speak evaporated. This was no octogenarian…and if she needed help driving her golf buggy around the green, he was taking up golf, pronto.

She was small and willowy, lissome of limb, and her eyes were divine, *more* than divine…sparkly and greenishly-hazel, and fringed with—

Whoa. He was sounding like a drunk English poet from a century long, long ago. Okay, the woman at the counter was a looker, in that girl-next-door way that had been weakening his knees ever since adolescence had kicked his hormones into full throttle. That was no reason to lose whatever was left of his common sense.

He tried again. "Can I help you, ma'am?"

"Oh, hi. I hope so. Wait! Is that…a mark on your face?"

He ran his hand over the slight graze running along his jaw. What was it with women and scars? "Ran into a brick wall," he said.

"I know. I was there."

She was *there?* He ran his eyes over her again. The woman in the pretty dress with the even prettier face, bore absolutely no resemblance to the shaggy gray dog he'd bowled over the weekend before. "No way."

She smiled, and it was like the clouds parted and sunshine shone for a moment on her, just her. "Sorry again for the, um, bump."

He was not sorry at all. If he was a romantic, like Jules, he'd be thinking fate had finally decided to take a hand in his life. Thank heavens he didn't own any embroidery thread.

She cleared her throat. "So, um…I'm looking for the cross-word writer you employ here, someone named, um…"

She colored faintly, and he raised an eyebrow. Sure, Tuna Yango was a heck of a nom-de-plume. He couldn't wait to hear it spill from her pretty lips.

"Yes?" he said helpfully. "Named…?"

She cleared her throat. "Tuna Yango."

He grinned. Who would have thought throwing in his career for a non-paying job at the local paper would be such fun? "You're looking at him."

Her eyes widened. "*You* write the cryptic crosswords in the *Cove to Coast Herald?*"

"Guilty as charged. Why, am I not what you expected?"

"I hadn't— I didn't— Well, heck."

Her blush was as adorable as the rest of her. Her reddish-blonde hair was pulled back in a loose braid, and the pink hair tie she'd wrapped the end of the plait in was a dead match for the color that fanned in her cheeks. He rested an elbow on the counter, suddenly understanding the appeal Jules and Danny found in chatting with customers for hours on end. If he'd had any reliance at all on the milk in the office fridge being within its due date, he'd have offered to make the vision before him a coffee.

She changed tacks, apparently giving up on trying to describe who she'd expected. "I need a bit of help."

"Sure. Anything." Had he said that too quickly? A year of finding no interest in anything besides his newspaper page, and now he was falling over himself trying to flirt with a woman who attended summer festivals in a dog suit? He had issues.

She smiled up at him gratefully, and if he hadn't been

smitten before, he sure as heck was now. "I'd be so grateful. The thing is, I'm terrible at games."

"You've come to the right place. I'm great at games."

"It's my sister. She's missing."

He frowned. "Um...like, missing in a game of Hide and Seek? Or actually missing?"

She shrugged. "The police don't think it's anything to worry about, but I need answers, even if the police don't. Which is why I've come here."

He glanced around the office. Okay, so their old-fashioned building could have mirrored a detective agency, with its desks piled with papers and its shelves crowded with books and broken cameras and spiralbound notebooks. But the clues he solved here had nothing to do with the real world.

He hesitated. Getting involved was not what he did—he was in retirement from all and everything—but his brain had just remembered what Dr. Goodly had suggested, that he find a project that made him feel uncomfortable and accept it.

Well, he felt uncomfortable all right, but he let his mouth do the talking before the cowardly part of his brain could intervene. "Maybe you could have a seat and tell me a bit more. I'm not quite understanding what sort of help I could be."

"Oh, could I? I'd be so grateful."

The look she bestowed on him cut a path straight through the fog of apathy he'd been living in for the last year and landed straight in his heart. "I'll do whatever I can," he said. And meant it.

"Are you okay with me having my dog inside?"

"No problem," he said, blithely ignoring the fact that he

had zero idea what the landlord's opinion of dogs indoors might be. "He need some water?"

"She. Her name's Rose."

He reached out a hand to shake hers. "Anton Price. Pleased to meet you."

"Katie Shields," she said. "Wait. Anton Price the *novelist?*"

"Former novelist. Current crossword creator cunningly disguising himself among the Redwood Cove community as Tuna Yango."

"That is seriously the weirdest name ever."

He grinned. "Sure, but there's a method to the madness. It's an anag—"

The dog stepped on his foot, and he looked down. "Hey, girl. What's up?"

The dog looked up at him and—he could have sworn it —winked.

"It's an anagra—"

The dog stood on his foot again, this time putting about fifty pounds of weight onto it.

"Rose!" said Katie. "I'm sorry, she's not usually so clumsy."

"No problem." He ushered Katie over to his desk and swept all the *Dear Anna* letters into the top drawer. Rose settled onto the floor by her owner's side, looking like butter wouldn't melt in her mouth.

Creative brains were the worst, he thought. Dogs were winking at him now? He really had to get a grip.

"So," he said. "Maybe we can start with why you think Tuna Yango can help you with your missing sister?"

She took a moment to speak. "Okay," she said. "You remember a year ago, when Redwood Cove was struggling with the economic downturn?"

Yeah, back when every news headline was like an arrow straight to his heart. Of course he remembered…hadn't his own darn novel predicted it? Become a runaway bestseller and filled him with guilt and self-doubt and an oversensitive panic reflex?

He cleared his throat. As beautiful as this visitor was, perhaps he should have let Danny or Jules deal with this. His therapist was wrong; he wasn't ready to leave the safe rut of his anonymity. "I remember."

"We—that is, my sister Veronica and me—lived with our Uncle Roly then. He'd looked after us since our parents died when we were little."

"I'm sorry for your loss."

She smiled at him gently, and he felt a little of his angst slide away. Wow. If he'd known the therapeutic results of a pretty smile earlier, maybe he'd have stopped hiding away in his cliffside cottage.

"I'm rambling, I'm sorry," she said. "Short version: Uncle Roly and Vee loved puzzles and games, that sort of thing."

"Games."

"Yes. And he and Vee used to work on the crossword page together in the *Cove to Coast Herald*. It was something they…well, sorry, I seem to be giving you my life history."

"I'm in no hurry." Which was true. Anton hadn't been in a hurry since he'd tossed his last manuscript into the hundred-year-old fireplace in his restored cottage.

Her fingers were twisting themselves into knots around the lead she had clutched in her hand, and he suddenly clued in to how stressed she was. Enough of his flippancy—the woman really wanted help.

"Just tell me the important bits," he said.

She smiled at him, and he felt his heart go loop-de-loop, which was amazing for two reasons. One, since when did sweet women track him down and ask for his assistance, and two, when had his heart last beat with anything other than resignation?

"Fast forward a few months after Uncle Roly passed away, and Veronica moved to Maple Ridge. She had this kooky idea that one way for her and me to keep in touch was to write each other a letter each week and she'd teach me how to do a crossword clue."

"And her letters have stopped arriving? Is that what's happened?"

"I got one last Friday, same as always, which is kinda why the police think I'm overreacting. But this week's didn't arrive, and she's not answering her calls, and she's not at her apartment. It's what the first letter said that has brought me to you."

He waited.

"She wrote in it, *Thank heavens for Tuna Yango LOL.*"

He sat back in his chair. "Huh. I can see why you came here. Anything else in the letter?"

"Just that she'd been keeping something from me for a while now, the fact that the reason she moved towns wasn't so much for the promotion it offered but to get away from someone at her work she'd had a crush on. And now she wasn't embarrassed about that anymore, because she'd met someone. THE someone. And then the line, *thank heavens for Tuna Yango.*"

"LOL," he muttered.

"Excuse me?"

"The first time you said it, you said 'LOL'... that's exactly what she wrote?"

"Yes, that's right."

He pulled a pen towards him and found a notepad so he could write down the phrase. Tuna Yango was definitely him. LOL meant laugh out loud. Thank heavens? No idea.

"Veronica, you say. Veronica Shields? Same surname as you?"

"Yes."

He pulled his laptop towards him. "It's not ringing any bells, but I'll do a content search in my columns since I took over the page a year ago, see if it pops up."

He typed the letters out into a search string and hit go.

*No results found*, his laptop blinked back at him.

"No luck. I'm kind of at a loss. Does she look like you?" Because boy howdy, he was pretty sure he'd remember if someone who looked like Katie had passed within hailing distance.

"A little. Here, I'll show you a photo."

He waited while she scrolled through her phone until she'd hit on the Reel Life app. A stream of photos popped up, and she tapped one so it filled the screen, then leaned in closer to the desk to show him. A waft of spring flowers and sea breeze lifted from her hair, and it took a second to remember he was supposed to be being helpful here. He looked at the two women smiling out from the screen.

Katie was wearing a bright yellow dress, a sleeveless summer number that showed off her tanned arms. In her hands she held a posy of hot pink flowers...carnations, perhaps. Beside her smiled a taller, blonder version of her. Jawline a little squarer, expression less sweet, but definitely a

KEEPING KATIE                    49

sister. They made a lovely pair, and he knew without a doubt he'd never laid eyes on Veronica.

"Can you send me that?" he said. "Danny—he's the owner of the newspaper—and his sidekick, Julia, are the ones who are here in the office every day. If your sister ever came in here, they're the ones to ask."

"Sure," she said. "Can I add you on Reel Life?"

"I don't have an account, but I run the newspaper's. Share it as a private message, and I can show it to Danny and Jules."

"Okay." She sounded despondent. "I can't think of any reason why she would have mentioned Tuna Yango. It's just so *weird*."

He shrugged. "She'd been sharing crossword clues with you for a while, you said. Could it have anything to do with them?"

Her eyes widened. "Well, heck! Maybe. I wonder—"

She came to a stop and held a hand to her mouth.

"You look as though you're having a brainstorm."

She smiled. "Not quite a full-on brainy moment. The opposite, actually. The thing is…she thought I was trying to solve all the clues she was sending me. She'd give me little tips. You know, thinking I'd just arrive at the answer, but I suck at these things. Truly. What if the crossword clue had some meaning in it that I just didn't get?"

"Maybe." It seemed a total longshot, but hey, who was he to understand the intricacies of a random woman's brain? "Which clue was it?"

"I should have brought the envelope with me. Do you have the last few Saturday papers here?"

He grinned. "Only about a hundred copies. Sure, let me grab some from out back. Umm…" He hesitated. What if she took off while he was gone? What if this was the only time he'd see her? Some long dormant drive for action had stirred itself into wakefulness when Katie Shields walked into the office of the *Cove to Coast Herald*, and he wasn't ready to let it go back to sleep. "There'll be a pot of coffee out back. Would you like a cup?"

"Oh, heavens, yes," she said. "Black, no sugar. Strong enough to land a jumbo jet on."

He grinned. Oh, yeah. Katie had woken him up all right.

# CHAPTER 9

*K*atie rested a hand on Rose's head as the cryptic crossword guy headed through a swing door and disappeared out of sight.

"Anton Price!" she whispered into the fur between Rose's ears. "I can't believe I didn't recognize him last weekend. He is *famous*." Like, possibly Redwood Cove's most famous resident after Finch Jameson and Hawk Hawkins. And famous was just one thing about him that had stopped her heart in its tracks. If she'd known how Hollywood hero the local crossword compiler looked, she'd have put in a lot more effort into working out those kooky clues her sister was obsessed with.

Dark, sun-streaked hair, the sort that you had to earn with long hours spent on a surfboard or swimming vigorous lengths of the cove. Shoulders that looked more suited to crushing granite or felling cedar than plying a trade on a keyboard. And those eyes! Dark, like the color thrilling secrets would be, if thrilling secrets were a soft-centered chocolate.

She glanced down at her dog. "I'm not delusional, am I, Rose? The guy's a looker, right?"

Rose stood up on her back paws, looked over Anton's messy desk, and casually knocked a pile of his business cards onto Katie's lap.

Katie frowned at her dog. "What, you're psychic now? Well, you're wrong. I do not need to know some random hot guy's contact details. I'm here for some help, then I'll be on my way." She waited until the dog had flopped back to the floor before discreetly sliding a business card into one of the credit-card slots in her phone cover.

She'd shivered her way through all of his books over the years...usually tucked up under a thick quilt, her bedside lamp burning deep into the night as she read about secret agents defusing missile launchers and data analysts foiling global economic bank heists. Anton could write!

She wondered what on earth had led him to give it all up to work here, on an ancient desk in an equally ancient building in the white-washed timber tourist district of Redwood Cove.

When he shouldered his way back through the doors, he was carrying a stack of newspapers under his arm and a huge mug in each hand. "No cookies," he reported. "You want goodies around here, you need to keep a secret stash in the janitor's closet, which is the one place guaranteed to never be disturbed."

She laughed. "The refuge kitchen is like that. You're more likely to find liver treats in the goodie-jar than a chocolate-chunk cookie."

"Oh, you work at the refuge?"

She grinned. "You think I dress up like a dog for fun? Of course I work at the refuge. We were fundraising at the festival, which was why I was lurking in dark alleys dressed in a lot of gray fur."

"That's pretty inspiring."

"Thanks. I volunteer there a couple of times a week—and it's more Rose's gig than mine. She's a therapy dog for animals who've been diagnosed with fear-aggression, which limits their chances of being re-homed. Rose is their last chance for redemption. She's very patient, and she lets them learn how to get closer to her in a gradual way. We build up to play, tug-o-war, that sort of thing. If we get to the point where I can take the troubled dog for a walk through the park with other dogs around, then we know we can try to find a suitable home."

"I am so impressed."

She smiled. Helping dogs survive a fear-aggression problem was her vocation, but the reason for that wasn't something she ever felt the need to talk about. "It makes a change from my day job. I work in traffic control at the airport, which is very exact, all numbers and vectors and graphs. Training the dogs gives me as much therapy as the dogs receive, because it's such a different way of using your brain."

"I bet."

"I'm sorry, I rattle on when I'm nervous. You find last week's newspaper?"

"I found a few back issues. Here's crossword 2086. Any of these clues ring a bell?"

She pulled the newspaper around so she could read the list. "Oh yes, this one's familiar. Here, *thirteen across, six letters. My twin initially, she is sweet to every relative.*"

"Sister."

"Um...that's right, we're looking for my sister."

"No. The answer to that clue is sister. This is one of the easy clues I put in each week to help the beginners fill some squares in the grid. It's an initial letter clue. She is sweet to every relative...the first letter of each of those words spells sister."

She looked blankly at the words in the clue. "I didn't see it. I must be the dumbest person alive."

He smiled. "Honey, if you can keep planes spinning about in the air without crashing into each other all day long, I'm pretty sure you're not the dumbest person in this room. See the word *initially?*"

"I see it." Did she sound defensive? She felt like she was back in grade school explaining to Mrs. Stilton that she really *did* know the difference between a noun and a verb.

His hand rested on hers for a fraction of a second. "It's totally fine. Brains work in different ways. Don't worry about fathoming the answers; that's why I'm here. The interesting thing about this clue is that it is sort of relevant. Maybe we *should* keep going."

She felt a blush warming her cheeks for some silly reason that probably belonged back in grade school along with her noun and verb lessons. "Thanks for the answer. I would never have worked it out."

"I can give you the answer grid for the whole crossword, if you think that would help?"

She shook her head. "I don't know, Anton. We only ever worked on the one clue, you know?"

He pulled the stack of papers towards him. "We'll go backwards, then. I'll pull out the crossword, you circle the clue that your sister sent you. Maybe we'll see some kind of pattern."

"I guess. Sure." It was a plan, and she sure didn't have any other suggestions to offer. They got to work, Anton tearing out *Page Seventeen* of every Saturday issue, and her circling the clues she could remember with a fat red pen.

"Read them out," he said, when they'd gone back three months.

"*Three down, six letters: Help! One who profanes wildly,*" she read.

"Rescue."

"Hang on a minute, I'll write that on my list. Okay, next up is *one across, five letters: Love from afar? More space needed.*"

"Crush."

She rolled her eyes. Seriously, people wasted their Saturdays on this stuff? She wrote it on the page and turned to the next crossword. "*Twelve across, seven letters: In California, color would, we hear, suit state symbol.*"

Anton looked at her. "Come on, this is an easy one. Know any state symbols for California...?"

She looked at his expectant face. "Nope. I've got nothing."

He smiled. "Redwood."

"Redwood? I'm not even going to try and fathom how you got that. Let's see, what have we got. Sister, redwood, crush, rescue. Could be gobbledygook, could be totally menacing."

He shook his head. "I'm sorry, Katie. These clues are so random, I'm really struggling to think how any of this could be helpful in finding your sister."

"It's got to help, because I'm all out of options."

"You checked with all her usual gal pals?"

"Yep."

"Old school friends? Old boyfriends?"

"Yes, checked."

"Distant cousins? Godparents? The batty great-aunt you only ever see at Thanksgiving?"

"If we had any of the above, I'd have checked with them. Thorough, aren't you?"

He smiled. "*So* thorough."

How had he managed to turn that into a comment which did a slow burn through her nerve endings? She took a breath. Focus, Katie, *focus*. She sighed. It had been a crazy idea coming down here, and now she was getting distracted by warm brown eyes and a fine set of shoulders. She took a swig of coffee from the giant mug and winced. "Eesh."

"Lukewarm?" He raised his eyebrows at her in sympathy.

"Like my heart—"

Oh, shoot. She'd nearly said that out loud! She slammed the mug back down on the desk and stood, tugging on Rose's lead as she did so. "I've taken up enough of your time. Thank you."

He stood, too. "No problem. I'm sorry I couldn't be more help. Hey, let me know if you find your sister, will you? Tuna Yango will want to know. I can...er, pass on the message."

"Sure, fine, yes," she stammered, and took off back to the street, only stopping to breathe when the timber-and-glass door had thunked to a close behind her.

She pressed a hand to her chest, alarmed and thrilled in equal measure that her heart, for the first time in a long time, didn't feel lukewarm at all.

Too bad she didn't have time to wonder what that meant. She had a sister to find, and it seemed Tuna Yango was going to be too big of a distraction to be any help.

# CHAPTER 10

*A*nton spent a thoughtful week.

He jogged—alone like always—and wondered what it would be like to have someone jogging beside him. He worked his way through the R section of his secondhand cookbook—rice pilaf, risotto *con fungi*, rolled chicken stuffed with brie and pancetta—and imagined a woman standing beside him, helping herself to a sip from his glass of wine, sampling the bubbling pot of risotto to test if the rice was *al dente*.

It had been a long, long time since he'd pictured living a life with someone else in it...and now that someone had a face. He frowned at himself in the gilt mirror above his hall table. "For a guy who doesn't believe in love at first sight, you're acting like a total sap, Price."

Still. Would it hurt to get a haircut? Spend more than thirty seconds picking out which shirt to wear in the morning?

Not that it mattered what shirt he was wearing, today or any day; his Monday afternoon visitor had probably returned home to find her sister on her doorstep or had received a dozen text messages, like *sorry, my phone died, all is well,* etcetera etcetera. Tuna Yango was just a distant memory to her by now.

He pushed his wandering thoughts aside. Even a semi-employed newspaper columnist like him had to work sometimes, and this was one of those times. He hauled his laptop out of its case and set off for the flagged patio that spilled out from his kitchen onto the rocky cliffside. Time to pick this week's selection for *Happy Snaps*. He logged into Reel Life and scrolled through the submissions. Lovely photos, many of them, but some a little blurred or bleached out. He stopped on one showing the sun rising over water. That wasn't a common sight here on the west coast of the States. Sunsets, sure...each night more spectacular than the one before. But sunrises?

He enlarged the photo to see if he could recognize any details. Of course—Lake Eloise. A picnic area and campground in the foothills of the Santa Lucia Mountains. He'd been there many a time, back when he was doing research for *The Garden of Evil*. He'd needed a lost hiker, a psychopath with an orienteering obsession, remote wilderness trails...

He shuddered. There was nothing to be gained in rehashing the macabre plots in his past. Whoever had taken this lovely photo of Lake Eloise had not had psycho killers in her mind. The photo was burnished with golden light. A bird —some sort of downy woodpecker—perched on a fallen tree limb, its wings a blur of movement. He should go out there one day, and replace all his research memories with this lovely one.

His phone bleeped as he dragged the photo over to a folder on his laptop for his next article, and he picked it up before

he'd quite computed that the words on the screen said
*unknown number calling.*

Hmm. He hoped his editor hadn't switched phones in an
effort to trick him into answering, because if he had, it had
just worked. He was wilier than a darn coyote.

"Oh, er, hi. Anton?"

His editor had a voice like a train derailing into a gravel
quarry...this was *so* not his editor on the line. This voice was
hummingbirds drunk on honey, faeries plucking strings on
golden harps, ange—

"Hello? It's Katie. We met last week in your office."

He cleared his throat. "Katie?"

"Yeah. I hope you don't mind me calling you so late."

Was it late? His adrenalin had just jumped him into a
never-ending wakeful dawn. "Not at all. Did you find your
sister?"

Her sigh dampened his thrill at hearing her voice. "No.
That's kind of why I'm calling."

"Oh." He scrambled for something to say. "Er...you need
my help again?"

"I just keep circling back to that letter she sent me. Her
crush on a suitable guy at work here at SantaCal Bank, her
meeting someone...and then thank heaven for Tuna Yango."

"It's a conundrum."

She had a smile in her voice when she answered. "Not a
word I'd ever think to use, but yeah. It's definitely a conundrum. Maybe we gave up too easily the other day with the
crossword clues."

"You want to go back a little further?"

"If you don't mind."

Mind? His hormones had just started singing the Hallelujah Chorus.

"And I think I'm going to have to go to Veronica's old workplace."

"Where? The bank?"

"Yes. I've been thinking about Vee's note. I just fastened on to the Tuna Yango thing because it stood out. What if something else in there was a clue?"

"You're sounding like a detective."

She chuckled in his ear, and the sound warmed him. "That is so unlikely, Anton. A lateral thinker I am not. There's a reason I became a traffic controller, not a...a...FBI agent. I'm a one-plus-one-equals-two kinda gal."

He tore his mind away from how much he liked hearing that deep chuckle of hers and how much more he'd like to hear it in person. "So what else does the letter have in it that you can work with?"

"Two things. First, is the guy she had a crush on here? Maybe I could find out who that person is and ask him if she's been in touch."

"Could be awkward."

"Yeah. I'm dreading it, to be honest. Since, um—well, let's just say making chitchat with people I don't know isn't one of my strengths. After that, I need to head on back to Maple Ridge and somehow ask her coworkers there if they know who this new guy is."

He waited a beat. "When are you thinking of following up these leads?"

"I'm on the dawn shift tomorrow at the airport, so I'm off duty at noon. I thought I'd swing into town on my way home and visit Vee's old branch on Main Street."

He instantly cleared his plans for the next afternoon—which wasn't, admittedly, difficult: he had no plans, not for tomorrow or any day. "Want to meet up first? I can print up the answer grids to all the Saturday crosswords we didn't get to, so you have the answers on hand."

"Oh."

She fell silent, and he tried to interpret the inflection in that softly spoken *oh*. Was it *Oh, shoot, I've called a stalker, and he's probably a total crackpot?* Or was it more of an *oh, heavens, that hot dude with the murky past and the apathetic future just asked me out, and I'm a teeny-weeny bit thrilled?*

"I'd like that."

Wait, had she said that, or was his fertile brain filling in all the answers again? No, she'd definitely spoken, and now it was his turn. "You would?" He cleared his throat and brought his voice back down an octave. "How about the park above the beach? There's a cafe across the road that makes incredible donuts."

"Sweet and Treats? I love those donuts."

"I love that you love those donuts." Jiminy cricket, he needed to think about his conversational skills. He was losing it. L.O.S.I.N.G I.T.

"See you tomorrow, then?"

"Yeah," he said, and slid the phone back down onto the table. He lifted his gaze to where the setting sun was sending streaks of color through the sky in the direction of tomorrow, and smiled. For the first time in a long, long, time, he had something to look forward to.

# CHAPTER 11

*I love that you love those donuts*, Katie mused to herself as she found a parking lot near the town square and clipped Rose to her leash. "Do you think—?"

Rose trotted along the footpath beside her, looking up, waiting for her to finish the thought.

"Never mind. Enjoy your walk, my fluff. An hour or two in town, then we're heading out to the refuge for another session with Prince. How does that sound?"

Rose's nose had been distracted by a drooping fern which apparently needed to be disciplined, so Katie slowed while her dog batted at it with her front paws until it lay inanimate.

"You done? Because if you're finished, we have a man to meet."

Rose woofed.

"Correct, I did say a man."

Rose woofed again.

"Also correct; I did, not so long ago, say we would never get involved with a man ever again, but this is different." How different, she didn't yet know. She just knew that she had a spring in her step, the flowers were blooming pinker and brighter than they ought to be, and the sun felt like spun gold on her skin. Despite the fact that she was on a mission here—her sister could be *missing*, for Pete's sake—the prospect of meeting up with Anton for a donut had made her buoyantly happy.

The park running along this part of the coast was one of Katie's favorite places to laze away a few hours. Flowering allamanda grew over wrought-iron arbors. Low hedges of ixora lined the flagged pathways, and the wide, palm-fringed esplanade was home to a steady stream of joggers and stroller-pushing parents.

She couldn't see Anton, so she settled at a picnic table near the monument to health workers. *Service above self*, the deeply chiseled inscription read.

She stroked Rose's head. "Those wonderful people," she murmured. "And you are wonderful too, my sweet, every time you help one of those fear-filled pups escape Heartbreak Row."

"I should have bought three donuts."

She looked up, and there was Anton, smiling down at her and Rose. He'd lost the dark shadow that had clung to his jawline when they'd first met, and his hair had been shorn of its tousled, fairy-tale-prince-astride-a-noble-stallion look.

He set two coffee cups down on the wooden table, along with a shiny paper bag with the Sweet and Treats logo printed on the exterior.

"Hi," she said, in a regrettably breathless way.

"Hi."

His brown eyes had a way of looking that really *looked*. No wonder she'd been bowled over on her first meeting.

"Any news from Vee?" he said.

Despite her worry, she couldn't stop herself from grinning. Veronica used all four syllables of her name, and insisted everyone else did, too. Katie only got away with saying Vee because she was family. "No. Nothing. No phone messages, no posts on Reel Life, zip."

Anton settled into the bench seat beside her, so they were both looking out over the view. Rose shifted under the table so she could lie across their feet.

"Just nudge her away if you don't like dogs so close. She won't be offended."

He smiled. "I love dogs. I'd have one in a heartbeat if I didn't travel so mu—"

He came to a halt mid-word, and she slanted a glance up at him. "If you didn't travel so much?"

He gave her a sheepish grin. "Past tense. I guess I haven't been doing much of anything lately. I've been…giving myself a time-out."

"From travel?"

"From writing, mostly."

"For real? But people line up for your books."

"Yeah. So my agent keeps reminding me," he said, tearing the paper bag in half so a puff of warm, cinnamon-sugar goodness billowed up and her taste buds went into high alert.

"Oh my," she groaned. "I made a pact with myself: only one a month. This will be my third in a week."

"You've been stressed. Donuts are medicinal; it's a proven thing."

She took a bite from the warm, doughy chunk he handed to her. "If only that were true."

Rose gave a soft whiffle beneath the table.

"Is it okay if I give her some?" said Anton.

"Sure, but just a bit so she doesn't feel left out. And it'll have to be our little secret. If Carol, the breeder who gave me Rose, ever found out, she'd stage an intervention."

"Ouch. Sounds a bit like Jules at the newspaper. Since she found out I'd given up writing, she's been sending me books about curing writer's block and leaving little embroidered scraps of cloth on my desk with self-help sayings. *Take your mind out and dance on it, Mark Twain*, that kind of thing."

Katie took a sip of her coffee. "That is so adorable. Hand-sewn? Who even knows how to do that anymore? She must care for you a lot; I hope your wife doesn't get jealous."

Oh, wow. She'd wondered at his single-or-not status, and somehow her mouth had thought it would be okay to just ask away, without checking with her brain first.

Was she imagining the little twinkle in his eye as he looked at her? "There's no wife or girlfriend to care about who's stitching me little notes."

"Huh," she said.

"How about you? Anyone in your life who's going to worry about who you're, um…sharing donuts with?"

"Besides Rose? No. There was someone, a few months ago, but I don't think I was reading the signals very well."

"How do you mean?"

"You know how I said I was a literal thinker? A one-plus-one-equals-two girl? Well, I thought our dates were going somewhere, but Jetson thought I was too…" Too what? He'd accused her of being too inward-looking, too unwilling to take chances and be impulsive. She'd been trying, and he'd just mocked her and then taken off.

She sighed. "Whatever he thought, he didn't stick around

to see if it was true. He found a job in a bigger city and took off for a more glamorous future."

"Wow. Jetson. Please tell me he was embarrassed by that name."

She giggled. All those months of feeling bad about the way she and Jetson had ended things evaporated in the face of Anton's ridiculous comment. "He thought it was captivating. Bond...Jetson Bond, that sort of thing."

"I have never wished so badly to be a rom-com writer. That man deserves to be immortalized as the dopey moron who let the best girl he'd ever meet get away."

Katie buried her nose in the lid of her coffee cup. Was that a compliment? Or just a bit of fun? She glanced up, and Anton's eyes met hers. Warmly. So warmly, in fact, that she felt a little tremor of longing that she hadn't felt in... well...ever.

She cleared her throat. This was no time to be losing her focus just because kind brown eyes were giving her the come-hithers. "So, er, I think you were going to give me the answer grids to all the crosswords you—well, Tuna Yango—published in the *Cove to Coast Herald*."

"I've got them here. I had another idea, too. Say no if you don't like it, okay? It's just...I might have a bit of clout at the local SantaCal Bank branch. If you want me to come with you so we can work out who your sister might have been in contact with, I'm happy to help."

"You are?" He was? Oh heck, she could spin her brain cells into a lather wondering, or she could just ask. "Why do you want to help me, Anton?"

He spent a long time looking over the waves breaking on the point before he answered, and when the words started, they weren't quite what she expected.

"You know I said I'd given up writing?"

"Mmhmm."

"It wasn't the whole story. Truth is, for a while there, I gave up on pretty much everything. Getting up. Buying groceries. Answering my phone."

She rested her hand on his arm. "I'm sorry, Anton. Did you lose someone?"

He placed his hand over hers, and she tried to remember she was comforting someone; these little trills of reaction were *so* not appropriate.

"No. It wasn't what I lost. It's what I had done."

She frowned. "What did you do? Sneeze over strangers at the drugstore? Hoard rice?"

He squeezed her hand. "Huh. I'm beginning to see why Veronica may have wanted to give you the slip."

She grinned. "Seriously, Anton. What on earth would you have to feel guilty about?"

"My last book."

She sorted through titles in her head, trying to think which might have been the most recent. She was a fan, sure, but not a rabid one. She didn't have his book titles tattooed across her breast. "Er...*Delta Echo Nine? Nevada Storm?*"

"*Strain X.*"

"I haven't read it."

"Well, you must be the only person in the Northern Hemisphere. Sold more copies than all my other books put together, which was great, and my ego grew into something about the size of Alaska. But then—"

He broke off, and she could see what it cost him to choke down what he was feeling. "But then it all became real?"

He nodded. "Yeah. The world went crazy, and I couldn't get over the fact that I'd been fictionalizing pain and fear and worry on a global scale...and profiting off it. I started having panic attacks, so I stepped away."

She mulled over his words. "I'm not getting the link between your book and helping me."

He snuck another piece of donut under the table to Rose, who would be ecstatic to find she now had an undisciplined treat-giver in her life. "I've been using the newspaper page I'm in charge of as a means of sticking to a routine, keeping involved in a minor way...but it's not enough. It's time I stopped sulking"—he turned to her and raised his eyebrows —"which is what my sisters tell me I'm doing, and reconnect with the world. Helping you find your sister feels like the nudge out the door I've been needing."

"A nudge, huh." That didn't sound romantic at all. She was surprised at how disappointed that made her feel. Still, he was a fiend with crossword clues, and he used to write mystery novels for a living...he had to be better at solving the case of her missing sister than she would be on her own.

"I'm not sure how I feel about you using my sister to push yourself out of your sulk-fest."

He winced. "Ouch. Was that insensitive? I'm sorry. I'm a bit out of practice."

She smiled. "However ..."

"Yes?"

"I am going to magnanimously allow you to accompany me to SantaCal and throw your celebrity writer status around."

He grinned. "You need me."

"I need my sister," she said, loving the way he totally

understood when she was being serious and when she was being facetious. "You are just a tool."

"I am cool with that," he said. "It's nice to feel useful."

She frowned. "Hey, Anton, about you feeling guilty about profiting off your book, *Strain X*. I'm sorry you had to go through that."

It was his turn to frown this time. "Katie, you've got nothing to be sorry for."

She raised her eyebrows at him. "And neither do you, Nostradamus. You wrote a book, not a prophecy. Stuff happens, okay? It happens, we deal with it, we move on wiser and kinder."

He snuck another piece of donut under the table into Rose's mouth as though Katie wasn't totally aware of what he was doing. "I know you're right...but sometimes knowing something in your head and knowing something in your heart can seem like totally different things. Anyway, enough about me, the point is that I'm ready to emerge out of my time-out. Your sister did mention my penname in her letter, so I'm thinking now may be my chance to use my creative skills for good instead of—"

"Don't say evil. That would be both melodramatic and untrue."

He winked at her. "I'm a tad partial to melodrama. It goes hand in hand with a creative brain."

She bumped her shoulder against his. "I'm a tad partial to cold, hard reality. It goes hand in hand with a logical brain."

"Sounds like we make a great team, Katie Shields."

Yeah. Sounds like, she thought. "Okay," she said.

"Okay?"

"Let's go to the bank, hotshot. You can wow me with your mad bank-teller schmoozing skills."

She took a deep breath as she gathered Rose's lead into her hands and followed her new mystery-solving buddy across the thick, trimmed turf. Yeah. As though she hadn't already had the socks wowed off her already.

# CHAPTER 12

"I'd like to make a transfer of some funds, Cath," Anton said to the manager of the Main Street branch of SantaCal Bank.

"Of course. Why don't we take this into my office? Your friend can take a seat—oh, I'm sorry, ma'am, we don't allow dogs in the bank."

"She's a therapy dog," said Katie beside him. "I have a license to bring her into buildings; here, let me get it out of my purse."

Cath took a second look at the massive golden girl sitting neatly at Katie's feet. "Oh my. Don't tell me she's one of Carol Graves' dogs?"

"That's right."

"She must be related to my grandson's Boris. My grandson has epilepsy, and Boris has changed that little man's life for the better. Your dog is welcome, young lady. Thank you for explaining."

"Er...thanks."

"Now, are you happy to take a seat while Anton and I transact his business?"

"She can come with us," he cut in. "It's fine."

"Of course. This way."

Anton winked at Katie. Cath had been looking after his deposits here since he was a teenager, banking his first paycheck from the seafood restaurant where he'd bused tables. Of course, Cath had been a teller than. And a brunette, if he remembered rightly. She'd called him *sir* back when he was a gangly fifteen-year-old with the confidence of a tadpole, and he'd puffed up proud as a bullfrog. Today, she was a silver-haired, silver-tongued branch manager with an enviable reputation for business acumen.

"Haven't seen you lately, Anton," Cath said as she settled herself behind her desk. "Been hidden away in your study cranking out your next masterpiece, I expect."

He shot a sideways glance at Katie. "Something like that. Look, I got you back here on false pretenses."

Cath raised her eyebrows. "Oh, this is exciting. Is this for your plot? Do you need some inside banking knowledge? How many inches thick is the steel door of our safe? How many alarms we have in the building, that sort of thing?"

He chuckled. "Not quite. We're um...more interested in how many young single men of dating age you might have employed here."

If the bank manager's eyebrows rose any higher, they were going to disappear into her stylish silver pixie-cut. "I don't understand."

He looked over at Katie for help.

"Cath," said Katie. "You must know my sister, Veronica Shields."

"Well, now I know why you look a little familiar. I don't think I caught your name."

"Katie, Katie Shields. I'm trying to track Veronica down."

"She hasn't worked here for months. She moved out to head up the loans department at Maple Ridge."

"Yes. I know. But she's taken some personal leave and didn't let me know where she was going, and I'm trying to find out where she might be."

"And with whom," cut in Anton.

Cath looked perplexed. "I don't know how I can help."

"Vee, I mean Veronica, told me she was a little involved with one of the guys on staff here. She said it ended awkwardly. We're hoping to find out who he might be so we can ask him if he's heard from her."

Cath sat back in her chair, her hands steepled in front of her. He saw the moment she figured out who the guy was that Katie's sister had been involved with.

"Come on, Cath," he said. "Let's have his name."

She pursed her lips. "I can't give it to you."

He frowned. "Why not?"

"Privacy rules, of course."

Katie stirred beside him. "Cath, I'm worried about my sister. I've tried every avenue I can think of to get in touch with her, and she's nowhere. I've checked her home, her workplace, the new gym she goes to. No one's seen her. It's not like her to not respond like this."

"Look, I can see you're worried. Here's what I *can* do. I will contact the person in question. Do you have a number you can give me? If he's happy to talk to you, he can give you a call."

Anton looked at Katie. It was a good outcome, even if it

meant the frustration of not being able to question the guy right this second.

Katie pulled a card from her purse and handed it over to the bank manager. "Thank you, Cath. I appreciate it."

"No problem. I can send your sister a message via our internal system too, if you like. Nothing that will get her in trouble with management...just a suggestion she give me a call when she gets a moment. That way, in case she is checking her work messages, I can let her know you've been in looking for her."

"Thank you."

THE SPRING that had been in Katie's step earlier in the day had well and truly rusted itself stiff.

"Looks like our interrogation will have to wait," Anton said.

"I shouldn't have built my hopes up." Katie sighed.

"Cath will make contact. We're further ahead now than we were an hour ago."

"You're right, I know. I'm just feeling a bit blue about it."

Feeling blue was something he totally got. "I might have a remedy for that."

"Yes?" She looked up at him, and he felt a surge of protectiveness. He'd be putting his hand under her arm to support her down the street any second now if he didn't get a grip. This was the modern world, not some nineteenth-century drama.

He steered their footsteps away from Main Street and in the direction of the narrow headland that formed the southern rim of the cove. The cliff walk began in just a hundred yards, and there was something he wanted to show her.

"I'm not sure if you've seen the photo section of my page in the *Cove to Coast Herald*," he began.

"Sure I have. Beach views, mountain views, garden views. People pick an image from their Reel Life account and share what it is about that local spot that makes them feel good."

"Yes. Okay, so...I have a little secret—and it's only slightly creepy."

She chuckled, and he noticed a little of that spring was back. "Only slightly? Does creepy have a graded scale?"

"Sometimes I try and find where the photo was taken. I stand exactly where I think the photographer stood, and I try to feel what the photographer felt. A few months ago, they were some of the only happy moments I had, imagining being someone else." He hoped he wasn't oversharing. Maybe he was being arrogant, thinking a washed-up thriller writer with a barely remembered psychology degree could offer support to anyone.

"Oh, Anton."

It took him a moment to work out that she'd put her arm under his. *She* was supporting *him* as they walked the scenic track. How he loved the modern world.

"Take a look," he said.

Before them, beyond the guardrail that separated the cliff edge from the walking path, roared the Pacific Ocean. From the lookout on the headland, the full force of ocean rollers swept by, unfettered by the shallows of the bay. White seafoam flew from the waves, and gulls skimmed, wings outstretched, from crest to crest.

"*Photo by David*," he quoted. "My third instalment of *Happy Snaps*. He wrote in to tell me he'd walked here every day for three months after he was released from Gold Coast General Hospital after a car accident. His injuries were so bad his medical team weren't sure he would walk, so when he could... he came here to celebrate it, every single day."

Katie's arm was still firmly tucked under his, and Rose had looped around to his other side, so he was bound there, between them, held firm.

"Huh," she said. "That's a lovely thing for him to share."

"It's hard to imagine, isn't it, being so grateful to be able to use your legs."

Her eyes were on the distant horizon. "His relief, his pride, his excitement... I think I understand why you find these photographs so comforting, Anton. I have a view of my own that I spend time with when I need to take a moment. Sometimes I go there when I'm happy. Sometimes I go there when I'm sad. Something about the scope of it, the scale of a view that has mountains and oceans, farmland and city...it helps me find perspective, I think. The world is bigger than me and my thoughts. Sometimes I need to remember that."

He took in a long, salty breath and blamed the hot sting in his eyes on the sharp breeze. "Where is this view of yours?"

She smiled. "Nowhere you could go to see it. The control tower has an observation deck, a hundred feet above the runways. It's magic there...but it's a magic only authorized personnel can access."

"Take a photo someday, would you?"

"Someday," she murmured.

"I think I'm beginning to understand that you and Rose must be a formidable team in the therapy department."

Her shoulder was warm against his. "We try. Sometimes it's not enough, but we keep trying anyway."

She was right. Trying mattered...so why had he just given up? The world wouldn't crumble if he failed, and nor would he. For the first time in a long, long time, he thought about placing his fingertips on his keyboard, and typing out those scary, thrilling words...*Chapter One.*

# CHAPTER 13

Thursday, Katie worked the long shift and had no time for the refuge, no time for Prince, and precious little time for Rose. Thursday was supposed to be a half-day but turned into a full shift when Fabiana called in sick. She was slammed at work—the summer tourist season was heating up and joy flights to spot whales or visit vine-yards seemed to be on every visitor's agenda.

Joy flights. Who could deny anyone the simple joy of watching whales breach in the pristine waters off the Cali-fornian coast? Certainly not her, even when she was near dizzy with recording flight vectors and approach angles and runway line positions.

She'd worked late into the night reading every single one of Anton's—well, Tuna Yango's—crossword clues and answers, hoping to see something, anything, that made sense.

She'd learned nothing—not about her sister or about how to solve these pesky black-and-white grids that everyone she knew seemed obsessed with.

"The wife's sent in a hummingbird cake, Katie. Might want

to help yourself to a slice before the vultures pick the Tupperware dry," said Andy over her shoulder.

She dropped her pencil. "Not the one with the caramelized coconut shreds clinging to the sides? The cream-cheese icing with a hint of lemon?"

"That's the one. My Carmelita bakes like an angel. Better get into the staff kitchen."

Katie glanced at her watch. Lunch had been a long, long time ago, but the staff kitchen was gossip central, and casual chatter was about as easy for her to decode as crossword clues. All those *how are you*, and *haven't seen you*, and *what are you doing on the weekend* comments which she found so difficult to answer. "I'm off in five minutes, Andy. If there's any left, I'll wrap it up and take it with me. Peanut-butter-and-jelly sandwiches followed by a slice of Carmelita's cake sounds about the best dinner I can think of."

"Oh, Katie. Fabiana called, says she really wants to make up for her lost hours. You want a day off tomorrow? You can have it."

"Oh Andy! I would, thank you!" A whole day! She could drive up to Maple Ridge and go and stand at the Police Department enquiries desk and ask—no, *insist*—that they take her missing person complaint seriously. She could stop by Vee's work and her apartment, maybe loiter around the neighborhood looking for curtains that twitched…that sort of thing.

She stepped out onto the observation deck as soon as she'd signed out, for once ignoring her favorite view in all the world, and texted Anton.

*Going on a stakeout tomorrow. Might be an all-day thing. Interested?*

His answer wasn't long in coming. She'd packed up the last piece of cake and was slipping it into her purse when her phone bleeped.

*At last, I get to dig out my trusty sidekick costume.*

She smiled. *I don't want to drag you away from your crossword clues.*

*Drag me, I insist. Can you pick me up from my place?*

*Sure. Seven a.m. too early for you?*

*That's perfect. The old lighthouse keeper's cottage, down on the southern headland. You'll need to punch in the code EricP to get through the driveway gate.*

The lighthouse keeper's cottage? Holy moly, Anton lived *there*? It was one of the most beautiful homes in Redwood Cove, and she could only imagine how amazing the views were.

*I'll have Rose with me, is that okay? She loves a road trip.*

*Why wouldn't it be okay?*

Jeepers, it would have been quicker to call. She could feel a repetitive strain injury coming on in her thumbs with all this texting. She took a breath, then hit the little telephone icon. Maybe she *could* do casual chatter with the right motivation.

His deep voice was saying hello in her ear a moment later.

"Rose has a thing for cats," she said by way of greeting. "If you're going to have a seventeen-year-old tabby snoozing in the sun on your front doorstep, I'll keep Rose in the car."

"Rose the wonder dog has a flaw? Well, well. Tell her to chill: there's no cat, tabby or otherwise."

"Great." That was all she had to say, so why wasn't she hanging up already? Because she didn't want to, that's why. "So." She cleared her throat. "EricP? You named your door code after someone?"

His chuckle did something thrilling to her eardrum. "Crossword nut, remember? Anagrams are my favorite thing. EricP is an anagram of Price."

"Anton Price." It seemed weird saying a name she had seen emblazoned over half a dozen books on Uncle Roly's shelves.

"I know, right? It's like my name doesn't belong to me anymore."

She giggled. "Tuna Yango better not be your fallback position. That name is the worst."

"Ouch."

He didn't sound overly hurt. "Busy day?" Wow. Of all the lame conversation starters, that one had to be the lamest.

"The usual. Went for a run. Sorted out some photos for this week's news column. Turned to the letter G in my recipe book."

"Erm...you cook by letter?"

"Sure. G has a lot to offer a guy. Gnocchi, goat's cheese souffle, green beans, and gravy."

"Do you move to H after that?"

"Where would the fun be in that?"

"I guess," she heard herself murmur. Fun. When was the last time she'd just done something for fun? "I, er...I guess I'll see you soon."

"I'll be waiting."

Her phone beeped once as she was sliding it into her bag, and she checked the screen.

A message. From Anton.

X

X? X marks the spot? X as in the kiss mark you'd write at the end of a letter? Katie stared at her screen for a long second, then sighed and shoved her phone away out of sight.

If there was anything her last lackluster relationship had taught her, it was that she shouldn't jump to conclusions. She and Anton were mystery solving buddies...which, sure, was nice. It was *more* than nice. Were they friends? Yeah, it felt like they were moving towards friendship; the way Anton joked, the way she felt comfortable ribbing him...that was friendship wasn't it?

But this *other* thing she was feeling—this thrilling urgency to see him, talk to him, be near him—that was the undecipherable bit. The bit she was sure to get wrong, and the bit likely to do the most damage when he left. Like how everyone she loved always left.

Hauling out her car keys, Katie headed for the elevator and the long trip down to ground-level. Finding Veronica was what was important. Fun could wait. And so could deciphering all these unsettling Anton-and-Katie relationship clues.

# CHAPTER 14

*A*nton's alarm broke through his usual background noise of waves on rocks at the viciously early hour of five o'clock. He lay in the dark for a few seconds, wondering what in blazes had prompted him to set it for such a crazy time.

Oh! Katie, road trip, stakeout. That was why—not crazy alarm-setting, but hopeful alarm-setting.

He rolled out of bed and staggered to the walk-in closet that the architect had installed under the eaves of the sharply pitched roof, back when he'd had the cottage renovated to add a little twenty-first-century function to its nineteenth-century charm. He scratched at the beard that had grown in overnight. The shave could wait. A run, a coffee, and a scramble of something involving eggs and bacon and the chives that were taking over his micro veggie garden were first on the day's list of priorities.

He caught himself humming as he ran the track down from the cliff. The moon had disappeared, and the last of the stars were winking out as the ochre of a new day bloomed over the Santa Lucia mountain range to the south. A squirrel scampered across the road ahead of him as he turned away from town and headed along the coast road south. *Photo by Mizuki*, he thought at the crossroads, where a giant oak stood sentinel in the front garden of an old weatherboard house. One of the first photos he'd used in his *Happy Snaps* column. *Caught the school bus from right out front of that tree*, the man had written in his caption. *Fell out of it more times than I can count and held hands with a girl called Stacy once, which I wrote about in my diary for weeks. I took this photo a couple decades later when I came for my school reunion and posted it to my Reel Life account so I could remember it always. I feel like a happy ten-year-old every time I pass that tree.*

Anton slowed for a morning milk truck carrying a full load from one of the farm co-ops, and then he took an inland route home. The bakers were hard at work behind the frosted windows of Dessert First Bakery as he circled though town, and he could smell coffee beans roasting through the open doors of the cafés lining the esplanade. Redwood Cove was waking up, and he was waking up with it. His eye was caught by the shine of a well-loved slippery dip in the children's playground in the park. *Photo by Sasha*, he thought. *This playground is where my baby first said 'Mom'*.

Little things, he thought as he wound his way up the narrow, zig-zag track that led into his front garden. Little, imperfect memories added up one by one into a wonderful life. He hoped. Maybe that's what his *Happy Snaps* column had been teaching him all these months.

The morning run and the memories of other people whose little memories he'd envied were on his mind when Katie drove up to his front porch in a spectacularly battered hatchback...perhaps that was why he lifted his phone and snapped a photo as she stepped out of the driver's seat with a huge golden dog bulldozing her way out behind her.

Katie wore a yellow slip of a dress. Her hair was blowing about her face in the breeze lifting off the ocean, and the sun was making her skin glow.

A happy memory of his own. Hopefully the first of many.

"Hey," she said, smiling up at him, and it felt like the sun had risen twice that day, just for him.

He would have said hello back, but Rose rocketed up to his feet and sat on her haunches, lifting a paw. "Er...high five?"

The dog obliged by tapping his outstretched hand then disappearing into his house.

Katie's face switched from smiles to stricken. "Oh, I am so sorry, Anton. She doesn't normally barge into houses uninvited."

"It's fine. You want to come in for a bit?"

"Well..."

Her face was a picture of curiosity and embarrassment. He decided to let her off gently. "Don't worry, you're not the first person to want to check out my house. It is pretty special."

"Special?" Her voice was reverent. "It's stunning."

He held out his hand. "Come check out the terrace on the ocean side."

She slipped her fingers into his, and his morning rush to be ready all became worth it. He led her through the narrow passageway that opened out into the shared kitchen and living space and then through the wide French doors onto the terrace.

"Oh my word," she breathed.

"Yeah. I think that every time I sit here."

"The ocean! The birds, the sky…and these geraniums. Wow, my Uncle Roly would have gone nuts for these. He was a begonia man first, but geraniums were his second love."

"I water them, but I can't take more credit than that."

She dropped his hand to walk over to the old stone wall that circuited the narrow terrace and peer down to the bay below, where Redwood Cove's residents could be seen bustling about the streets and foreshore. "I could spend hours just people watching."

He could spend hours just watching her face.

"I love it, Anton."

He shrugged. "Thanks."

"This place was nearly a ruin when I was growing up here. When I was at high school, kids used to break in to check if there were ghosts here."

He smiled. "Yeah, I heard that. None so far."

She rested a hand on Rose's head, who had found her way out to them and sat neatly by her owner's side as though she'd never barged her way into a strange house in her life. He was beginning to suspect that Rose fancied herself a matchmaker. He'd have to invest in some rawhide snacks next time he was at the store…keep her on his team.

"I guess…we should head off?" Katie said.

"Sure. Let's go." If the day went well, and they were able to make contact with Veronica and set Katie's fears to rest, perhaps they could end the day here where they'd started it. On his terrace, the sunset spread out before them, sharing a— what random letter had he picked in his recipe book this week? V?—sharing a vindaloo, perhaps.

He settled himself in the tiny space of her hatchback passenger seat, ramming the seat back as far as it would go.

He could offer to take his car, which would fit him, Katie, and a family of golden retrievers, but this was her day. If playing sidekick meant scissoring himself into a space that hadn't been designed for a guy who'd used a basketball scholarship to get himself through college, he was cool with that.

"What's brought on the road trip?" he said as they spun through town and hit the coastal freeway. "Did you get a phone call from Vee's mystery crush at the local SantaCal branch?"

"No such luck. Andy—that's my boss at Redwood Cove Airport—offered me a day off from work today, so I thought I'd take the time to head on over to Maple Ridge and visit my sister's apartment, her place of work, and so on. The police department too."

"I'm sorry that lead didn't pan out."

"Yeah, me too. You know, I could have sworn your bank manager friend, Cath, knew who we were talking about."

"Totally. She practically had little cartoon lightbulbs in her eyes."

Katie took her eyes off the road to flash him a look. "I know, right?"

He checked his watch. 7.20 a.m. Early, but worth a shot anyway. He pulled out his phone and scrolled through his contacts. There she was, tucked neatly in between *Canton King Takeaway* and *Cavendish Road Publishers*. Hmm. Joe and Han, the proprietors of his local Chinese takeout store, he should put on speed dial. The other number—his publisher's number —he'd been avoiding. He let his eyes rest on Katie's face for a moment. She didn't know where her sister was, and she was worried, but instead of sticking her head in the sand and hoping it would all go away, she was hell-bent on finding answers, working on a solution to her problem.

Unlike him. His books—in particular the manuscript he was contracted to write but had written exactly zero words for—were a major problem, but he'd been the proverbial ostrich about them. Head down in the sand every time his publisher called.

Maybe he was ready to do something about that. What, he wasn't sure yet. But *something*.

After Katie found Veronica, and after he found a way to keep Katie in his life.

He set his fingertip fair and square over the words *Cath SantaCal* in his contacts list and held the phone to his ear as the ringing started.

"Cathy Baxter, SantaCal Bank, Redwood Cove branch."

"Cath, hi. Anton Price here."

"Anton. Calling before office hours, be still my beating heart. I assume you've finally caved to your inner need for a cougar in your life and want to ask me out on a date?"

He chuckled. Cath was as wedded to being a smart-mouthed, career-driven spinster as he was to his peaceful, ocean view terrace. "Nice one."

Her bantering tone switched a gear. "Is this about the matter you were in for the other day?"

"Yep. I don't want to pressure you—just wondered if you had anything you could legally tell me. We're running on empty here."

"I'm sorry. I spoke to Fra—um, the person who I think Veronica may have been hinting about, but he looked at me like I had rocks in my head when I suggested he give your friend a call. I don't think he has anything to do with Veronica, he says he barely knew her. Plus, he's been at work all week, and there have been no signs of lipstick on his collar, if you get my drift."

He sighed. "Okay, understood. Thanks Cath, I appreciate it."

"Anytime, Anton. Be sure to let me know when your new book's hitting the stores, won't you? I'm your biggest fan."

"I'm having a bit of a break, actually Cath." Wow. That was the first time he'd not prevaricated and just let the general public assume he was all systems go on the Anton Price blockbuster gravy train.

"Aw, Anton. You take the time you need. I'll just be looking forward to the next one even more. You tell that girl of yours I'll be calling her as soon as Fra—er, that person decides to be helpful."

"Sure. Thanks Cath." He dropped his phone into his lap and let his gaze rest on Katie—who wasn't his girl, not by a long shot.

She raised her eyebrows at him. "Nothing?"

"Whoever Vee had a crush on, his first name begins with an F, and then possibly an R."

"Fred? Fraser? Franco?"

"And…" This was the downer. "He's been at work all week and thought Cath was nuts when she suggested he knew your sister."

"Hmm." She tapped her fingers on the steering wheel. "That sounds like a dead end."

He smiled. "There's no such thing as dead ends when you're solving clues. We make a note, we move onto the next lead, and we circle back later if we need to."

She rolled her eyes. "Oh, man, is that the crossword guy

speaking? I have had the worst week wading through that stuff you gave me."

His hand had somehow or other found its way to a lock of hair dangling just below her ear. He wrapped it around his finger. "The worst week?" he murmured.

He could see her neck move when she cleared her throat. "Well, okay, that is an exaggeration. We've all had worse weeks. A tricky, sleep-deprived week, I should have said."

"You could have called me. I can decipher clues in my sleep."

"Said no normal person ever," she said.

He grinned. "Normal is overrated. Which clue got you riled up this bad?"

"Well, for starters, there was this inane one: *two down: Say no to trash.*"

"A classic two phrase, one meaning clue."

"Wow," she said. "Am I the only person in California who thinks these things are impossible? I am so not smart."

He wanted to sniff that lock of hair in his fingers so badly it was like an ache. "Untrue. You are one smart cookie, Katie Shields."

Rose gave a low woof from her spot tethered in the back seat, and he laughed. "Your dog agrees."

"She's biased. I feed her and let her sleep at the end of my bed. She is legally obliged to think I'm smart; it's in our dog ownership contract."

He reached back and rested his hand on Rose's head. "You and I are going to be great friends, Rosie girl."

He received a fat lick across his palm in agreement.

"So, what's step one in today's stakeout program?"

Katie looked at her watch. "Another hour or so until we're

in Maple Ridge. I thought we could try Vee's apartment first, then her work, then visit the Police Department."

"Okay. Let's do this."

Katie looked across at him. "I'm glad I don't have to do this alone."

He felt glad to be the one chosen to be her company. "Katie?"

"Yes?" Her voice had a little rush in it this time, that he hoped like heck meant he wasn't the only one feeling like all his tomorrows had just landed in his lap, if only he had the courage to accept them.

"When we find your sister?"

"Yes?"

"I'm still going to want to see you."

Her smile and the blush riding high across her cheekbone as she dragged her gaze back to the highway were enough to make him hope that she felt the same way.

# CHAPTER 15

*V*eronica's apartment was a bust. Katie made Anton stay on the sidewalk to keep his eyes on the windows while she pressed the buzzer beside the entry door.

"No movement," he called up.

She peered in through the glass door to where a curved set of stairs led upwards. A tattered umbrella lay abandoned in one corner, and a drooping cactus sheltered in another.

"Pity we can't get inside to bang on her door," she muttered as Anton came up the stairs beside her.

"That's your literal brain thinking," he said. "Allow me."

She watched in equal parts horror and awe as he pressed all the door buzzers, one after the other. After a second's pause, a deep voice cut through the intercom.

"If that's my pepperoni double cheese, bring it up to level three." The voice cut out, and the door buzzed. Anton gave it a nudge with two fingers, and the lock opened.

"Open sesame," he said.

"I can't believe that worked. Has that guy not seen *California Psycho?*"

"I don't think a guy who orders pizza for breakfast is overly concerned about being some psycho's fetish."

She sniffed. "Good point."

He grinned at her, and her not-so-icy heart did a little loop-de-loop. "Thriller Writing 101, Katie. Have a bold hero."

She tried for a flippant response, but that phrase, *bold hero*, had seized hold of her hormones and scrambled them into mush.

"What number is your sister's apartment?"

"Er...five. Up two flights."

She followed him up the stairs, trying very, very hard not to let her eyes find out whether he had a bold hero's butt. Focus, she reminded herself. *Focus!*

The door to Apartment Five was off-white, with two silver locks neatly inset above a chrome handle. No claw marks. No signs that an axe had ever gouged out chunks of timber in an attempt to break in...or out. As doors went, it was as bland as could be.

She knocked anyway, despite knowing in her heart that Vee wasn't there. No way could Vee be living there just ignoring all the messages Katie had left on her machine.

Silence followed her vigorous knock, only broken when the door opposite snapped open and an elderly woman with a tortoiseshell cat weaving in and out between her neat navy slippers asked them what on earth they were doing making such a racket just when she was trying to watch her show.

Katie didn't know who was more surprised: her and Anton, to finally gain access to someone they could question about Veronica's whereabouts, or Rose, who had spotted the cat and frozen into a state of pre-lunge readiness.

"Staaaaay," she ordered her dog in the alpha tone she used for just such cat emergencies. The fur on the back of Rose's neck quivered with the effort of being obedient. Katie shot a wild look at Anton.

"I'll take the dog," he said. Clearly, Thriller Writing 101 must include being able to size up a pressure cooker situation in a heartbeat and react. She smiled at him gratefully and passed the lead to him before turning to the woman.

"I'm so sorry," she said. "I'm Veronica's sister; she lives in number five. I haven't heard from her in a few days, and I'm a bit worried. You haven't seen her by any chance?"

The woman inspected Katie through her fancy, emerald-green eyeglasses. "You must be Katie."

"Oh, I am." Thank heavens, Vee and the lady must be a little acquainted.

"Well, Katie, I'll thank you to stop ringing your sister's phone all the hours of the day and the night. Her phone noise comes right out her window and floats straight into mine, and if I have to hear "It's me, Katie" again, I'm going to have six conniptions. I am eighty-three, young lady. I can't handle any more conniptions in my day."

Katie cleared her throat. So...not apartment neighbor buddies then. "Er, I'm sorry. Again. But can you please tell me if you've seen her?"

The neighbor's gaze narrowed. "Well, now I think on it, I did see her last weekend, running up and down these stairs making a racket like is not allowed in this building's by-laws."

A racket? "What sort of a racket?"

"Her and that fancy-pants man of hers. Nearly took out Pandora here with a ladder."

Katie dropped her eyes to the cat, who was sitting by the woman's navy slipper and looking up at her in that smug, unblinking way that cats had. "Nothing since then? No more…er, rackets or broken by-laws?"

"Are you giving me sass, young lady? I am eighty-three years old, and I do not take sass."

"No, ma'am," Katie said, suppressing her grin and wishing for the world that Anton hadn't missed this interchange.

"Then I have nothing more to say. Come, Pandora!"

KATIE WAS GIGGLING as she hauled open the door of her hatchback and rejoined Anton and Rose in the car.

"Good news, then?" said Anton.

She shrugged. "I don't know where Veronica is, so I'm not going to give up searching, but I think—I hope—that I can dial down my worry a little."

"The plot thickens. Please, explain."

"Apparently Vee and some fancy-pants man—that's a direct quote from the eighty-three-year-old dominatrix across the hall—were dragging renovation equipment up and down the stairwell last weekend."

"Renovation equipment?"

"Vee flips houses as a side hustle. It is totally in character for her to be carrying ladders and things up and down stairs."

"So we're looking maybe at a planned excursion somewhere, rather than alien abduction?"

She reached out to thump him in the arm for the alien

comment, then quickly withdrew her hand. *Focus, Katie,* she reminded herself. *Don't overreact, don't presume this relationship is something it isn't. You know you always get it wrong.*

She brought her mind back to what she was supposed to be thinking about. "I think so, yes, Anton. I can't tell you how relieved I feel. It still doesn't answer the questions of who she is with, or why she's not answering my calls or emails...but it's a happier set of facts than all the ones I've been imagining."

"Cool. Are we relieved enough to indulge in coffee before we hit her workplace for our next clue-busters campaign?"

"Coffee *and* cake. I'm buying."

She spun her head around to address Rose. "And *you'll* be pleased to know, my lamb, that Auntie Veronica's ladder used up one of that smug cat's nine lives last weekend."

Rose gave a satisfied woof.

# CHAPTER 16

*H*e took a photo of the mountains rising up above the town while Katie browsed through the knick-knacks for sale in the quaint café they found on the main street.

*Photo by Anton*, he imagined typesetting into his *Happy Snaps* column, if this photo ever popped up in the *Cove to Coast Herald's* Reel Life account. *This view makes me happy because it was taken the day I realized I was content, for the first time in months.* Content and happy and no longer so focused on regret.

He took another photo of the trellis in the small park near the café, where he and Rose spent a happy hour while Katie visited the local SantaCal Bank branch and the small police department. A climbing vine covered the trellis with triumphant orange flowers, and at its base, Rose snuffling along contentedly at the end of her lead.

*Photo by Rose the Golden*, he thought with a grin. *The place where my human's new friend took this photo rocked. Eight*

*different squirrels musta pooped here, maybe even a raccoon!*
*Heckin' great. Best. Park. Ever.*

When Katie joined them a little while later, she wasn't precisely as worry-free as her dog, but she'd lost the drawn look that had accompanied her since he'd first met her.

She looked…he breathed in, then out, as she walked across the trimmed lawn towards them…beautiful.

"Any news?" he asked, dragging himself back into the moment.

"The manager was pretty cagey. She confirmed Veronica was on leave, but I had to show her my driver's license to prove I was who I said I was. She wouldn't tell me when she was due back."

"So…nothing we don't already know."

"Mmm."

The twinkle in Katie's eye was telling him there was more. "Why are you looking so pleased with yourself."

She grinned. "Okay, you know how I'm lousy at games?"

"I know how you *think* you're lousy at games."

"Right…well, as I was waiting for the manager to come out of her office, I noticed there was a display rack for all the senior bank employees in the Central Coast region. So-and-so was employee of the month, so-and-so were running in the local half-marathon to raise funds for endangered wildlife and the bank had chipped in a thousand dollars, that sort of thing."

He wasn't sure where this was going, but it was clearly going somewhere.

Katie pulled a wad of paper from her purse and held them out. "Here. Business cards and pamphlets. We look through these, we may find out more. I spotted Veronica in a photo on the board dressed in the bank's half-marathon training T-shirt. Worth a shot, right?"

"Definitely. Let's find a picnic bench so we can spread these out."

An hour later, Katie's enthusiasm had dropped back a notch. "I never knew how little interest I had in banking until this very moment."

"Snap. Check out this guy's job description," he said, reading from one of the business cards fanned out across the weathered timber. "Creative Analyst and Marketing Digi-Optimizer. That's a mouthful to type out every time you need to send an email. Fraser Lopez-Rodgers must be a touch-typing whiz-kid."

Katie looked up. "Say his name again."

"Fraser Lopez-Rodgers."

"I wonder..." Katie broke off and pulled out her phone.

"You thinking this Fraser guy could be the employee Cath almost mentioned?"

"Could be, Anton. Didn't she say his name started with an F and an R? I'm going to see if our guy Mr. Lopez-Rodgers has any public social media accounts."

"It doesn't fit with what we know from Vee's letter. The mystery F-and-R guy works in Redwood Cove, not here."

"Maybe he's a mobile marketer and digi-whatsit. He could service all the branches in the area, maybe? Secretly adored Vee from afar in, hopefully, a non-creepy way? Aha, gotcha." Katie swiveled her phone around and showed him a picture. A big guy, dressed in suit and tie, stood holding a golfing trophy. "What do you think?"

"Right age bracket. Your sister got a type?"

Katie frowned. "You know, a couple of weeks ago I would

have said yes, I totally know the kind of guy my sister would be interested in. But now? Now I'm wondering what else she has kept from me. And why."

He kept her phone and swiped through a few more photos of their only candidate so far in the hunt for who Veronica Shields may have gone away with. "Oh. I don't think this is our guy."

"Why? What have you found?"

He spun the screen so Katie could see the next photo of the same big guy, but this time instead of a golf trophy, his arms were around a tiny woman in a silk kimono, and three scrubbed and pajama-clad youngsters were lined up in a row in front of them. "I think Fraser is already in the family way."

"Oh, no. Just when I thought we were getting somewhere."

He rested his hand on Katie's. "You know, we have no reason to believe there's any foul play going on. Your sister has taken official leave from work, her apartment neighbor saw her willingly carrying equipment up and down stairs with someone who was clearly a friend, not a stranger. Katie...the only reason you're worrying is that she's not answering her mobile phone. She could have lost it. She could have forgotten to take her charger."

Katie's shoulders shook, just a little, as she murmured, "But what if I need her?"

There. That was the clue *he'd* needed to understand what was really driving Katie to find Veronica. "I know we don't know each other that well, Katie...but while your sister's away, if you need someone, you know you can call me, right?"

She turned her head a little to the side. If she thought he couldn't see the tears that were fighting to break through, she was wrong.

She turned her hand over, and her fingers clasped his. After a second, she spoke, and her voice had an upbeat tone to it that rang a little forced. "For a has-been thriller writer, you're okay, Anton Price. But I'm not...I mean...what I'm trying to say is, I'm not in a position to be calling anyone. A man I mean. I'm not looking for that."

He stood up and pulled her to her feet. She was trying to be brave, and he could respect that, even if her words had sent a bolt of fear through his heart. Still, he hadn't gotten this far in life without learning that sometimes, patience was the best course of action. "Come on, why don't I drive us home and you can be off duty for a bit. We'll be home by lunch...maybe you could take the afternoon off from worry and relax a little."

"Yeah," she said. "Maybe."

# CHAPTER 17

*A* workout with Prince was exactly what Katie needed, the tougher the better after nearly crying in the park. Relaxing was so not on her agenda.

Okay, she had tried to relax, but ended up just moping about her house, beating herself up for saying those words to Anton.

He had been nothing but kind, and she had pushed him away.

She took the hint when Rose went and retrieved her therapy-dog harness from the laundry and dropped it on her feet.

Nothing worked so well to get her head out of the blues as working at helping someone else…or in this case, some dog. Rose was right. She could find a better use for her time than lying around on the sofa wondering why Veronica hadn't shared her plans with her.

After two hours working with Rose at the refuge, and with Prince growing more and more relaxed and confident, she walked the two of them on their leads up to the container office by the front gate. "I'm taking Prince to the dog park," she said to Ramon. "Would you mind if Rose kept you company in the office for an hour or so? If he acts up, I'm going to need both my hands free."

"Me and Rose? For sure. We've a batch of abandoned pups in Row A who are seriously in need of some life lessons in dog behavior. You okay with me taking her into meet them?"

"They had their shots?"

"Vaccinated, bathed, dewormed, deflead. The only things these pups have got left to call their own is their appetite."

She smiled. "Sure. Rose? Don't sneak one home. Uncle Roly's garden beds couldn't take another four-pawed hole-digger."

PRINCE CAME through with flying colors.

She didn't let him off the lead—she didn't think he'd ever settle down enough to become an off-leash dog, but he sailed past a dozen dogs without pulling on the lead, he kept his teeth hidden, his hackles down, and remembered how to sit on command even when dogs of all sizes and shapes were bounding around them.

Even a bumptious pug named Bossy didn't faze him. Bossy's owner apologized profusely as she dragged her barking bundle of fun away from Prince's tail.

"I'm so sorry. He never comes when I call."

Katie nodded. "It's a good command to work on. You see the yellow ribbon Prince has around his neck?"

"So pretty," said the woman. "I love that color on him."

Katie smiled. "A yellow ribbon means anxiety. It's a signal to other owners to keep their dogs away a little, just so Prince can take some time to check out all these experiences at the park without feeling pressured."

"I had no idea!"

"No problem; now you do. Hey, if you're ever interested in teaching Bossy how to come when he's called, the Gold Coast Dog Refuge out in the industrial precinct runs classes every now and then. It's not expensive. Me and a few other volunteer trainers run classes on weekends, and the fees go towards helping the refuge keep operating. I'd love to see you and Bossy there some time."

"We would love that. Thanks for letting me know."

Bossy was doing his ninja best to wriggle out of his owner's arms, so Katie judged it a prudent time to head back to the refuge. "Enjoy your walk."

"You too."

By the time she'd dropped Prince back to his kennel and pulled into the driveway of her home, the rush of achievement in helping the abandoned dog move one step further away from the peril of Heartbreak Row was waning. Rose was first out of the car and had her muzzle full of mail from the mailbox by the time Katie caught up.

She unlocked the door and pushed it open, and it felt like a big cloud of silence wafted out of the house and dumped itself all over her. She'd left that morning so full of hope for what she might achieve in Maple Ridge—finding Veronica—but now all she had was the uneasy sense that she had deeper trouble than a missing sister who couldn't contact her. She had a sister who wasn't missing at all…

"I should cook some dinner," she said to Rose, who had scampered down the hall ahead of her and tossed the mail haphazardly over the floor and sofa. "Or we could just bake a cake and eat it out of the pan and let the food pyramid go hang for a night. What do you say?"

Rose gave a giant huff and settled onto the floor, her back legs crooked backwards, and her front legs crooked forwards, so she looked like a giant golden bear rug. Her eyebrows were doing that frown thing as though she knew exactly what Katie was suggesting and didn't approve at all.

"Oh, all right. You win. Meat and greens it is."

She picked up the mail that Rose had dropped over the floor. Did she want a new credit card and a case of wine every month? No. Neighborhood watch pamphlets, mayoral election campaigning, a free month at her local gym…no, no, no.

She tossed the rest back on the table. The blue envelope with the handwritten scrawl that she'd been waiting so long to receive wasn't there. All that was left to fill her evening was that darned pile of cryptic crosswords that Anton had printed for her. She read the next clue on the list, *six across: the rap you sing on the couch.*

*What??* If she had to spend even a minute of her evening dissecting that, she was going to follow the lead of that eccentric woman in Vee's building and have six conniptions.

Andy was right. She was young, not eighty-three. She was single, she had all her teeth, *and* she had a job. What was she doing, spending her evenings alone with her dog, waiting for her older sister to send her a keep-busy letter?

What had Andy suggested? Karaoke was never going to happen, but his other suggestion? Not the baking, as tempting as wallowing in high-carb treats sounded. The *other* one. She pulled her phone out of her purse before her over-cautious self could intervene. She'd told Anton she wasn't looking for a man to call, but the words had been a lie. Truth was, she was worried about being hurt by someone else she'd grown close to, and that's why she had brushed him off.

Perhaps Anton had been right, too…she should give herself a break from worry.

He picked up on the second ring.

"Question. Do you know what a hipster white-wine spritzer is?"

"No, but I'm in."

"Esplanade? Thirty minutes? You know The Orca Bar and Taphouse with the wine barrel tables?"

"Done."

A laugh that was equal parts happiness and hysteria burst out of her when she put down the phone and looked at her dog. "Well, don't just lie there looking hungry, girlfriend. We've got a closet crisis to attend to. I just discovered my sister has a life that doesn't involve me, then I panicked and invited a hot, successful guy out for a drink, and—kaboom—I have no idea what to wear."

# CHAPTER 18

*R*yan Mulligan checked the reception bars on the screen of his phone. No bars. He tapped a finger on the internet app. No service, either. He grinned. Finally, finally, he'd be able to get some peace.

He tucked his phone into his back pocket, adjusted the holster he wore around his shoulder, and assessed the mounting pile of firewood he'd spent the last hour cutting. A few more, he thought. A storm was galloping in over Mount Shasta if he was reading that black cloud right, and he planned on riding it out by the fire in his newly acquired mountain cabin.

Alone. Gloriously alone. Just him, the fire, a beer or two—and not a reporter or police uniform in sight. Even the stray dog that had turned up at the cabin a time or two, looking for food and affection, had disappeared.

He swung the axe down into the log on the block, grunting with satisfaction as it cleaved along the grain. He was beginning to get the hang of this mountain life. Maybe he'd snare a rabbit later—toss it in a pot with some wild greens. He snorted. As if. A steak on the *grill and a spud in the microwave was about the limit of his culinary skills.*

*Chucking the last of the split logs onto the woodpile, he gathered a handful of kindling and headed over to the cabin's back porch. He took a glance around before he went in. From habit, mostly...old habits died hard for a cop who spent his on-duty hours hunting down the scum of the earth.*

ANTON FLEXED HIS FINGERS. He felt like a guitar player who'd woken from a coma and realized he could no longer play his favorite riff, because all the calluses he'd spent years acquiring had been lost.

But despite the stiffness, keystroke by keystroke, the words had been coming. Even more exciting had been the *ideas*. Notepads were sprawled over the dining room table, the kitchen counter, the floor of the old lamp-oil storage room that he'd had converted into a book-lined study.

And here was the kicker, the epiphany he'd had as he'd driven down the mountain pass that afternoon in Katie's little hatchback and seen the jewel-blue Pacific Ocean glittering up at him. Tenacity mattered. Not giving up mattered.

Katie had taught him that.

The fact that her sister may not even be missing wasn't the point...the point was that Katie needed answers, for reasons that he was only beginning to understand, and she wasn't giving up, so neither should he. If he could create a cryptic crossword, he could sure as heck find a way to write a thriller that didn't end in an apocalypse.

He looked at his watch. Six p.m. in California made it nine

p.m. in New York. He'd be pushing it to find anyone still at work, but hey, wasn't NYC the city that never slept?

He hit the numbers and waited while the ring tone buzzed three thousand miles eastward.

"Wait," a dry voice said in his ear. "Someone smack me. I must be delirious, because my phone screen is telling me Anton Price, my star recruit, has finally decided to call me."

Huh. Looked like his editor, Eduardo, hadn't lost his love of facetiousness. "Hi."

"Hi?" For a one syllable word, Eduardo managed to fling it around a few octaves. "You ignore all my calls and emails for near on a year, and all you can say is hi?"

He took a breath. "I'm sorry, man. I've been ... struggling."

"I know you have. That's why I've been so desperate to talk to you, Ant. Tell me everything. How are you? What can I do? You need me to come out there and butter your toast, I'm on the next plane."

Wow. Just...wow. He'd been expecting grief for not living up to his end of their publishing contract, not support.

"I started something today."

"What—like, a manuscript?"

"Yeah."

"That is so cool. But listen, Anton. If you need time, that's what you're getting. You are one of our stars, and sure, we love it when we can splash your stuff out over every store in America, because your readers love you, man. But if you're not ready, we can be patient."

"I appreciate it, Eduardo. It's nowhere near a thing yet, but I wanted to let you know."

"You take care, man. I'll be waiting to read a few chapters when you've figured it out. And stay in touch already!"

Anton let out an unsteady breath. The relief of knowing the whole of the management division of Cavendish Road Publishing weren't baying for his blood was huge. "I'll know in a few weeks if what I'm working on has enough juice in it to become a full-blown story."

"Just make sure I'm the first to know, that's all I'm asking."

The first? Anton's brain shifted into a vision of him on a long romantic walk over the headland with Katie, telling her the happy news that he'd rediscovered his mojo. "I can't promise you the first, but you've got dibs on the second, Eduardo."

"You got it."

He'd no sooner dropped his phone to the table when it buzzed again. Huh…seemed like he only had to think her name and there she was. Fate was finally singing a tune even tone-deaf guys like him could hum along to.

"Question," Katie's voice said in his ear. "Do you know what a hipster white-wine spritzer is?"

This seemed like one of those questions that a guy needed to get right the first go. "No," he ventured, "but I'm in."

"Esplanade? Thirty minutes? You know The Orca Bar and Taphouse with the wine barrel tables?"

Anton looked up to the stars wheeling through the northern sky. Oh yeah, fate was singing a song in his key tonight. "Done," he said.

TWO HOURS LATER, Anton was tipping the waiter who had brought over their second round of drinks and a cheese platter.

"How did you get into dog therapy work?" he said.

"Oh. Well there's a short version and a long version of that answer. Which do you want?"

"Both. Start with the long version."

"Bonnie. She was our chocolate Lab when we were kids. When she was about seven or eight, she became difficult to handle. She'd always been uneasy around other dogs, so we never let her off leash, but then she started breaking out of the garden, attacking dogs. It was awful."

"What was wrong with her?"

"Fear aggression, we think. Maybe she had some sort of dog dementia, I'm not sure. We tried obedience classes, dog whisperers, training. Me and Vee watched thousands of clips online on how to train your dog, and with us at home she was an angel."

"But not outside the home."

"Nope. After a few years where her behavior escalated, she got out one day when the gate wasn't shut properly. Ran down an elderly woman who was walking her dachshund. She didn't bite anyone, but she barked and snapped so bad the woman fell over and was injured."

"Katie, how awful."

"Yes. It was truly awful. Our vet came over and talked to us and Uncle Roly, but we knew rehoming wasn't an option. She's..."

Katie's voice had grown thick.

"You don't have to tell me."

"No, it's fine. Bonnie's safe in Uncle Roly's garden, under one of his rose bushes. She still gets a lot of love."

"Wow. And that's why you work with dogs with behavioral issues?"

"Yes. It depends on their age and their willingness to learn, of course."

"So, what's the short version?"

"Oh." She took a sip of her wine. "When I was on college break—I studied engineering up at Santa Cruz before I did my air traffic certification—I volunteered at the refuge. It was still in town then, before those premises were sold. I cleaned kennels, walked the dogs, bathed them, and so on. That's how I met Carol Graves."

"She's like some town legend according to Danny. He's the owner of the *Cove to Coast Herald*."

"Your boss?"

He grinned. "Kind of."

"That sounds like you have a story of your own. But yes, Carol is a legend in these parts. Her golden retriever litters are the most sought-after therapy dogs on the West Coast. I was lucky to be given the chance to own one."

"Rose?"

She smiled. "Rose. Speaking of, I should probably get home to her. She'll be wondering why there's no one on the couch sniffling over a Hallmark channel movie."

He laughed. "I did not have you pegged as someone who cries at movies."

"Huh. Well, you'd be wrong."

"I love being wrong from time to time. For example, I was pretty sure that after this morning in the park, you had decided not to see me again. I'm pretty happy I was wrong about that."

She picked up a cardboard coaster with an orca embossed in the center and commenced tearing it into shreds. "I decided to take a chance."

He pulled the shreds of cardboard from her fingers and held her hand with his. "I'm glad. This has been fun. Let's do it again real soon, but with dinner."

She smiled up at him. "I'd like that. But um, yeah...I'd better get going."

"Did you drive? Because," he grinned, "hipster spritzers and safe driving practices don't seem a credible combination."

"It's fine," she said. "I walked. Uncle Roly's place isn't far; twenty minutes, tops." She waved her hand vaguely in the air, which did nothing to clear up the mystery of where her house might be.

"Come on, I'll walk you home."

"It's the opposite way from your place! I'll be fine, really."

"Thriller Writing 101," he said. "Things go bump in the night, so why risk it? Besides, I'd *like* to walk you home. I've been thinking about how I'm going to engineer the right moment for a boy-likes-girl kiss, and saying goodbye at your porch seems like the perfect place."

"You get pretty cocky after two spritzers, Price."

He grinned. "Not at all. Humble but hopeful."

Her giggle wrapped around him more warmly than a scarf ever could. "Come on, then. It's this way."

He fell into step beside her. "What are your thoughts on holding hands while we walk home?"

"I'm not sure," she said.

He waited a beat, then felt her smaller hand slide into his. He gave it a squeeze, and kept on walking. Baby steps.

Katie's house was a spic-and-span bungalow from a different era. Seeing the wide-planked porch and the shingled roof, he was reminded of the family shows he'd grown up watching on the television, where kids played in tree houses and old guys called Pops or Mister dispensed sage advice about growing up from the open door of their garages.

"Um...here we are."

He leaned down to find the catch on the low gate that led into the garden and creaked it open.

"What a lovely home," he said.

"It belongs to me and Veronica, has for over a year now, but I still think of it as Uncle Roly's place."

"Why is that, I wonder?"

She shrugged, and he let it go. Psychology could wait. The stars were out, and he could smell jasmine blooming somewhere in the garden.

A low woof sounded from behind the wide front door.

"Your chaperone," he said. "Does she start flicking the porch light on and off when your goodbyes linger too long?"

She raised her eyes to his. "Let's find out."

# CHAPTER 19

*K*atie took a sharp breath. Had those words just come out of her own mouth? Who was she, and what had the world done to the old Katie Shields, whose ex-boyfriends accused her of having a tepid heart?

Anton looked even more surprised than she was, which made her grin and gave her the courage to put her money where her mouth wa—

No, wait. Her mouth where her mou—

No, shoot, that didn't work either, but she stopped worrying about what was working and what wasn't, because she'd just stood on her tiptoes and pressed the fleetest of kisses on Anton's mouth, and he had let out a sigh that did something funny to her head.

And her heart.

And just about every nerve-ending she owned.

"Anton?" she breathed.

But he didn't say anything, he just gripped her shoulders in his big, wide hands and hauled her up against him and fastened his mouth to hers.

Oh, boy. Her heart wasn't lukewarm. It was made of thunder and galloping hooves and trees lashed by hurricanes and tiny dancing fairy lights that made spirals in an ink-blue sky...

The woof from behind the old wooden door was louder this time and was accompanied by a thud. Katie looked up as Anton lifted his face from hers.

"Wow," she said.

"That's a double wow from me."

"I'd, er, better, um...gosh."

His grin was sending her a lot of messages in that moment, fun and rakishness and an element of something too warm to be interpreted right that very second, with her thoughts in such disarray.

"Just what I was thinking."

She fumbled behind her for the lock, promptly dropping her purse to the ground and spilling the contents everywhere. "Uh, my keys."

Anton fished them from the pile and unlocked the door, to the delight of Rose, who barreled out, licked their hands madly for a second, then ran for her favorite patch of lawn.

"I'll get going," he said, and bent down to help her gather all her bits and pieces. Their hands met on a peach-colored lipstick, and she could feel her cheeks flushing a shade way darker than peach. She shoveled everything back into her purse and stood up.

"So, er...goodnight." Would he want to see her again? Should she suggest coffee? She had to work all week and Prince to train...when would suit her? When would suit him? Boy howdy, this man-woman business was hard. Andy had no idea how lucky he was to have snagged his sweetheart while he was still in the schoolyard, before all the pesky self-doubt of adulthood crippled his dreams.

Rose trotted back up the steps, then pounced on a folded sheet of paper lying on the front door mat and pushed it into Anton's hand.

"I think this is from your purse," he said.

"Oh! Yes. This is the letter my sister sent me, you know, the one that brought me haring into the *Cove to Coast Herald* looking for Tuna Yango."

"My lucky day," he said.

She laughed. "I don't know what possessed you to choose that ridiculous pen name."

He quirked his eyebrow at her. "But...I thought you knew?"

She frowned. "Knew what?"

"It's an anagram."

An anagram. Well, that would explain why it was so wacky. "Wait. At the risk of sounding even dumber than I must already seem...an anagram of what?"

He chuckled, and for some reason it made her both angry and sad. Anger won out. She didn't get games, was that a crime? Did it make her a bad person?

"This is so not funny, Anton."

His laughter faded. "Of course it's not. It's just a little embarrassing."

Her anger fanned into a sharp jab of hurt. "You think I'm embarrassing?"

"What? No! Embarrassing for me. Look, Tuna Yango is an anagram of Agony Aunt. When I took over the crossword in the newspaper, Danny—that's the owner—he coerced me into taking over the whole of *Page Seventeen*. Crossword, personal letters column, and the local photography section. I was up for the crosswords and photography, but he wouldn't let me ditch the personal letters section. Said it was the only thing half the people in this town read. I felt a bit dumb about being known as the local agony aunt, so I made up anagrams. Agony Aunt became Tuna Yango for the crossword, and Anna Toguy for the letters. *Dear Anna*, people say when they write in." He shrugged, six foot three inches of embarrassed male right there in front of her. "Do I look like a *Dear Anna* to you?"

He didn't, not at all. He looked like a handsome writing celebrity with the brain of a supercomputer, who had made it big in life and was now standing on her porch in one huge mistake. Her mistake.

A thought even bigger than the mistake standing in front of her made her gasp. "Oh my."

"What?"

She ripped open the letter she held in her hand and skimmed over the scrawl of her sister's writing.

*HEY THERE, sis!*

*This week's clue is a tricky anagram. You'll crack this one, I know you will. Five across...you know what to do!*

YADA YADA YADA. She fast-tracked her way down to the relevant section.

*I'VE MET SOMEONE. THE someone. I'm feeling so, so good about this, Katie. Like, the luckiest girl in the world. And to think it was Tuna*

*Yango who helped me out, LOL!!! Gotta love the irony of getting personal life hacks from a crossword compiler!*

*Call me for the details too juicy to put in print (\*waggles eyebrows up and down).*

*Vee xx*

"I HAVE BEEN SO STUPID," she breathed.

"How?"

She shoved the letter at him. "Read this paragraph. What does that say to you?"

She watched as he scanned the page. What had taken her nearly two weeks to work out took him about two nanoseconds. Go figure.

"We've been looking in the wrong place," he said. "It's not the crosswords Vee was saying had helped her out...it was the personal letters column."

"I'll need to look in those back issues again."

"Of course. I can put a bundle together straight away."

She took a breath. She'd grown carried away with all this missing-sister, clue-solving drama. Her ex-boyfriend had been right when he'd said she'd closed off her heart...she'd done so for a reason. Vee was—probably—not missing. Vee was just living her own life and was tired of having her needy, overly dependent little sister acting as a handbrake, so she had gone on holiday and not bothered telling her.

She needed to accept who she was. Katie Shields, loner, who worked and helped dogs and didn't do relationships very well. Not with her sister, that was now clear...and certainly not with someone so creative and lateral thinking as Anton.

The past days had been fun. More than fun. Better to stop

it now before she broke her thawing heart into even more pieces.

"If you could leave a pile of them at the newspaper office for me to collect, I'd be grateful."

"Sure, I can be there tomorrow. What time is best for you; do you have a work shift?"

She rested a hand on Rose's head for strength. "Just leave them at the counter. My schedule's pretty busy for the next little while. I can't commit to a time."

He looked at her for a long moment, then nodded. "I'll leave a package at the desk. Um, Katie, if I've said anything to upse—"

"You haven't." She was upset with herself, not with him. "I'd, er, better get inside; it's late. Uncle Roly's neighbors will be wondering what all the noise is about."

He walked down the steps to the path, then looked up. "Katie?"

"Yes?"

"You sure you're okay?"

She didn't have an answer. She just knew she felt—smaller, somehow, by what had happened here on the front stairs. And the last person she needed to see how small she was feeling was Anton.

"Goodnight," she said.

"Goodnight. The package will be waiting when you're ready to collect it. Take all the time you need."

She walked slowly into the house.

"Rose?" she said.

The dog rested a warm muzzle in her outstretched palm.

"Why do I get the feeling he wasn't just talking about the newspapers?"

# CHAPTER 20

*A*nton jogged through the mist that had swirled up off the ocean.

The minutes before the dawn were the most precious of the day, he'd always thought. They held the breath before the speech, the quiet before the chaos...and today, those fingers of light streaking up through the shadow of yesterday's nightfall had shone some clarity onto the conundrum which had kept him awake.

What, exactly, had he said to Katie that had turned a blissful goodnight kiss on her front porch into her closing him out?

The clues to the crossword. That had been the moment. She had been deeply sensitive to the fact that she struggled with word games, and he had blundered into that vulnerability like a bear into a picnic basket.

Good one, Price. The one good thing that's happened to you in a year, and you've blown it by finding it *funny*.

He turned a corner and let the thud, thud, thud of his sneakers smacking on asphalt fill his brain.

If there was anyone who hadn't worked out the clues, it had been him. He'd been so busy in his own headspace, he hadn't seen the hints right there in front of him.

He turned them over in his head as he ran. If only his intern job at the Psychology Department of San Diego General Hospital hadn't been so long ago, maybe he wouldn't have been so blind.

He tried to remember what he'd been trained to observe by his supervisor when a client came in for a session. The Fabulous Five, she'd called them, her signposts of a healthy mindset. Be in the moment, be kind to yourself, practice self-observation, stay physically healthy...heck. One more. Maybe he could ring Alice Goodly and ask her...let her know how splendidly his "say yes to an unexpected invitation" plan was going.

It came to him as he turned into the walking track above the beach, where he could see a few other early risers taking their morning walk. Couples mostly, holding hands and leaning into each other against the cool of the sea breeze. He sighed. Of course, that was the fifth: make and maintain healthy relationships.

Instead of taking the cliff walk up to the lighthouse and letting himself into his garden, he took the turn back into Redwood Cove.

He wasn't the only one who had been feeling disconnected or who had been looking for some sort of anchor to tether them back to the now.

His disconnect had been his writing. The subject matter of his last book had been the cause of his angst, and the royalties that had flowed into the bank account he could no longer stomach looking at.

Katie's disconnect? He wasn't sure, but he could guess. She missed her sister, that much he did know. She was lonely, like he had been lonely. She had her dog, Rose, and her work at the refuge, but were they enough?

The incline rose as he hit Main Street, and he turned the corner into the historic district when he reached the gracious old storefront that housed Simmons and Simmons Attorneys. With luck, Danny and Jules had left the spare key to the office in the bougainvillea pot by the front door. He had a year's worth of agony aunt columns to review. Battle stations, as his nephews would say.

He found the spare key hidden in the blow hole of a chipped pottery whale and ran his fingers over the cold hard metal. What was *his* anchor?

How many of the Fabulous Five could he tick off in the checklist of life?

He had his weekly page in the *Cove to Coast Herald*, but how often did he prepare it all at home, alone, rather than here in the office? Danny and Jules welcomed him like their long-lost prodigal son whenever he turned up, but how often had he invited them to his place in the last year?

Never.

Eduardo, he'd been evading.

School and college friends, there were plenty of those who'd welcome him into their homes if he called them, but that was the rub. If he called.

And when did he?

He hadn't cut his sisters out of his life, but his sisters didn't live in Redwood Cove. So long as they didn't visit in person, he could convince them he was happy and connected.

And that had been enough, until he met Katie.

Now, he'd realized the truth. Convincing himself and others he was happy was a terrible second best to *actually* being happy.

He'd found Katie, even when he hadn't known he was looking, and she'd given him the jolt he needed. He had his love of writing fiction back, and he had Katie to thank for that. Her dogged determination to find her sister had been the reboot his brain had needed.

He had a new friend who called him out of the blue and dragged him on stakeout missions to mountain towns. Took him on last-minute expeditions to a cozy wine bar at the end of the day. Held his hand.

He owed her everything, and he'd gone and blown it.

HE FOUND the letter shortly after lunch on Monday, after a weekend of wading through thousands of letters.

"Bingo," he said, just as Jules, who had turned up for work at nine, was trying to persuade him to eat half of her sandwich.

"I couldn't, Jules. You eat it. I'll grab something from Joe at the bakery."

"You'll take a half-pastrami-on-rye or feel the heat of my wrath, young man," she said, ignoring his protests and plunking a chipped plate on the desk next to him. "Now. You going to tell me what's got you going through all these old issues like you're digging for lost treasure?"

"I think this is the one I've been looking for," he said, scanning the page as he ate. "You got a minute to listen?"

"For you? Of course."

Julia perched herself up on the spare desk like she was a schoolgirl, not the grandmother she was. "Let's hear it."

*"Dear Anna,"* he read aloud.

*I've got a problem, and it's been festering in my head and making me unhappy, so I thought I would write for advice.*

*Here's the thing. I met someone, and I'm pretty sure this guy is the one, not just some foolish crush (that's a whole other story! #understatement). Problem is, I'm worried how my getting involved with someone, really involved, will affect my sister.*

*The man that raised us passed away a year ago, and we've been really close ever since. I had to move away from work, and my sister got really sad and quiet. Now if I start making time for someone else in my life, will that make her even more sad?*

*If I had to choose, I'd choose her.*

*But Anna...I really don't want to have to choose.*

*Yours,*

*Very Secretive*

THE INITIALS WERE the clue that had hit him right in the center of his crossword-solving synapses. VS for Very Secretive, and VS for Veronica Shields?

"What did Anna write in response?" said Julia.

He dropped his eyes to his response, half dreading what he might have written. Could there be anyone less qualified to answer agony aunt letters than a semi-depressed former psychologist who wrote high-octane thriller dramas for a living?

DEAR VERY SECRETIVE,

*You don't have to choose between your sister and yourself, but you do need to be thoughtful.*

*Now is not the time to be writing letters to Agony Aunts. Now is the time to be sitting down with your sister and talking to her about what you feel and what she feels.*

*People process grief in different ways, and some people need more help than others to make their way through.*

*Talk and listen. Then talk and listen some more. There are counselors here in Redwood Cove who can help you both.*

*But Very Secretive? If this guy is important to you, then you owe it to yourself to try to make it work. You matter too.*

*Yours,*

*Anna Toguy*

HMM. Not reckless, but cautious. As advice went, it was okay.

Jules eyed him over her grass-green spectacles. "Nicely said. What's the problem? Someone complained?"

"No."

"You going to make me drag this out of you, Anton? Because I've got all day. I can sit here, swinging my pretty little ankles as long as it takes. Tell Jules what's wrong."

He smiled at her. "You're not going to start embroidering me any more feel-good tips, are you?"

"I'll embroider what I like when I like, young man. Now come on." She dropped the bantering tone and frowned at him. "What's got you going through all these old letters?"

He sighed. "I've met someone."

"Oh, pet," said Jules, clasping her hands together. "Wait—is it this Very Secretive person?"

"No. Her sister."

"I see."

"She—Katie—is a little prickly. I think I offended her the other day, and now I've just found this letter from her sister which will upset her even more."

"That does sound like a pickle."

He chuckled. "A pickle? Now I know why Danny didn't make you take over the *Dear Anna* column."

She grinned. "Oh, he tried, pet. I just know a lot more than you about making Danny do things my way."

"Huh."

"Besides, I don't have a degree in psychology."

"I might have the piece of paper, but that's as far as my psychology career ever went, Jules, I can assure you."

She nodded. "You know what else I know, Anton? You're a nice guy. A *kind* guy. And I'm going to give you a little bit of agony aunt advice of my own."

He sat back in his chair. "I'm all ears."

"Now is the time to be sitting down with your young lady and talking to her about what you feel, and what she feels."

"Huh," he said again. "Sounds kinda neat when you say it."

She smiled at him and hoisted herself off the desk. "It'll come up nice on my next embroidery project, too," she said with a wink.

Talking it over. Telling Katie about his own issues, learning more about hers. If this was what it took for him to keep Katie in his life, then so be it.

Trouble was, first he had to show her this letter her sister had written. Whether she would be open to listening to him after that was a whole different ballgame.

# CHAPTER 21

*K*atie spent the week high in her control tower, trying to ignore everything in the world below her that didn't need clearance to land on a Redwood Cove Airport runway.

When Saturday came around, however, there was no work to keep her mind occupied.

Andy had refused to give her a shift. "Go home," he'd said as he waved her off on the Friday night. She'd gone home, she'd slept poorly, and now she was awake so early that she had to step over a snoring mound of golden fur to get out of her bedroom.

Okay, she'd overreacted last Friday night.

First, Anton had been adorable—fun at drinks, making her laugh the whole way home, making her feel like *she* was fun. too. Then he'd kissed her until she melted into a puddle of feelings that were new and warm and sweet.

But then he'd laughed.

Not at her. He'd explained that. He wasn't laughing at her ineptness at word games, and she knew it down deep.

She just overreacted anyway. She'd made the classic response every animal she and Rose had been training for the last few years had made when presented with a situation that made them anxious.

Fight or flight. And she'd chosen flight in the quickest way she'd known how, by brushing Anton off and racing inside her front door and slamming it shut while her heart hammered in her chest.

She spent the day on a beanbag in the den binge-watching cooking shows on television. By mid-afternoon, when it was time to head out to the pet refuge, she could have chopped a purple cabbage in sixty-three different ways, but she still had no idea what she was going to do about the stuff going on in her head.

Sunday was a little more productive; she took the dog for a swim down at Pebble Beach, threw the frisbee for her in the dog park until they were both out of breath, then spent the afternoon pushing Uncle Roly's ancient lawnmower up and down the lawns.

She should have done some housework too but settled on picking up the various dog toys that were scattered about. "That counts as housework, right, Rose?" she said, as she shoved her hand under the sofa to retrieve the long rubber alligator that Rose was partial to squeaking.

Her fingers closed over a smooth corner that didn't feel at all like Mr. Squeaky.

An envelope—a blue envelope—with her sister's hand-writing tripping across the front. *Katie Shields, 47 Prospect Road, Redwood Cove.*

What?

She twisted so she was in a sitting position, then tore it

open.


*KATIE,*

*Just a quick note this week, sorry, I'm a little pressed for time. You know that guy I was telling you about? Well (\*squee) Pete and I are running away for a few days to Santa Clara County to check out a house auction. He has zero experience with flipping houses, but he assures me he'll be excellent at holding my purse while I crawl around the rafters with my measuring tape.*

*The realtor says mobile reception is pretty patchy up there (something about mountains and cell-towers and bureaucracy) so if you don't hear from me for ten days or so, no need to call out the National Guard, lol!*

*Here's your clue for the week: four down, nine letters: pin shapes together for a laugh.*

*Hot tip: jumble two of the words up to find the answer.*

*Maybe when we get back you could come up for the weekend and meet Pete? I'm so hoping the two of you will get along.*

*Love as always,*

*Vee xx*

*P.S. Hugs for Rose*


KATIE LOOKED for a date on the letter, but found none. The envelope had a smudge of black ink that looked more like hieroglyphics than any readable date stamp.

"How did I miss this, Rose?"

The dog woofed and rolled onto her back in case a tummy scratch might answer the question. "Nice try," she said. Her hand was on the soft belly of her dog when she remembered who had been bringing in her mail recently.

Rose had. In her jaws, then dropping the pile onto whatever surface was close at hand. Vee's letter must have slipped under the sofa and been lurking there for over a week!

Her sister wasn't missing at all, just...away. Happy, gone, adventuring with her new friend, Pete.

Why, oh why, did everything suddenly seem so much worse?

Wait. If this was posted all that time ago, then that meant now, Sunday evening, her sister should be getting home.

She looked at her phone. At the risk of giving Veronica's neighbor a seventh conniption, she was going to have to call again. Hitting the numbers, she waited while the phone rang. And rang. And ra—

"Pete speaking."

She froze. She needed Vee, and she needed her now, not some random guy that she'd never even met. "This is Katie Shields speaking." Now she sounded like Vee's pursed-up, prim and persnickety spinster aunt.

"Katie! Well, hi."

He sounded warm. Nice. Like a guy who would hold a purse so his girlfriend could dirty herself up inspecting derelict houses. Darn it, why couldn't he have sounded like an evil mastermind that she could resent wholeheartedly?

"Um, is Veronica there?"

"She's just gone down to the store to get a new phone. There's a long and funny story for another day, but the short version is that I backed over her old one."

"You backed over—"

"Yep. As punishment, I get to cook every night for eternity, apparently."

"You're sounding right at home there, Pete."

"Er…is that a problem?"

Of course it wasn't, so why did she want to yell *yes, yes, yes* into the phone. Rose must have sensed her distress, because she came and lay—all seventy pounds of her—in Katie's lap.

"No," she lied. "Can you ask her to give me a call when she gets home?"

"Of course. It's so nice to talk to you in person, Katie. Vee's told me so much about you, and about Rose your beautiful dog, and about Uncle Roly's house, I can't wait to—"

"My house," she said.

"Excuse me?"

"It's *my* house. I'll be pleased to welcome you, Pete, when Veronica brings you to visit. Goodnight."

She put down the phone, and Rose lifted her head and regarded her with calm brown eyes.

"What?" she said.

Rose twitched her eyebrows.

"I know. I was a teeny-weeny bit rude. But at the end there?"

Rose looked up at her expectantly.

"At the end, I was magnificent."

# CHAPTER 22

*K*eeping Katie was his number one priority. After that came his skeleton of a manuscript which was slowly beginning to acquire some muscle and heart. Low on the list, but still needing to be done, he mused, frowning down at his layout for the upcoming Saturday edition of *Page Seventeen,* was working out some way of squeezing his clue, *money order from Prague, we hear,* into his crossword grid.

Aha! Two down, perfect. The solution had been staring him in the face, he just needed to see it.

An idea struck him. Another solution was staring him in the face, too...only this one didn't come neatly boxed in a black-and-white frame.

This one was wild. Epically wild. Wild and wondrous and —yeah, he could admit it without even feeling the tiny bit emasculated—desperate.

What did Katie care about?

Him. He was sure of it. He was willing to lay his heart on the line for it.

But she also cared about the animals on Heartbreak Row that she and her dog, Rose, trained every week in the hopes of rehabilitating them for a better life. And that was something he had the wherewithal to do something about.

If Katie really didn't care for him, he'd deal with it, and move on, and know that he'd done something good with the profits he had struggled so hard to deal with in past months.

But if she did care for him? At the very least, he'd have proven to her that he really did care. He really did respect her for who she was and how important her volunteer work was for the community.

THE TEMPORARY FACILITY of the dog refuge was worse than he'd expected. Clean, sure. Organized, spacious, and with outdoor dog runs neatly fenced off. But where were the fields? The shady trees, the cozy barn, the farmyard bliss that he realized, now, he'd been recalling from some Hollywood series he must have seen as a kid, where the sun was always shining and seven brawny brothers were busy swinging their seven comely brides in a dance routine through the hay bales.

Heartbreak Row had no Hollywood soundtrack to relieve the starkness of its chain-link fence, its cement flooring, its sad-eyed canine residents.

"We're always looking for donors," said Ramon, the volunteer who had been manning the office when he drove in. "We had premises on the south side up until a year ago, but the Mayor's Office needed to rezone them for development, and all we could get in a hurry was this unused industrial precinct. The Dorma Valley Winery owns the land and lets us use it for free, which is a heck of a fine thing considering the taxes they must pay...but still. You can see how unsuited it is for kennels."

"Tell me," Anton said. "If you could have your dream location, what would it look like?"

Ramon's smile would have done an orthodontist advertisement proud. "Five acres. No more than an hour from town so the volunteers can still man the place without finding the distance too much of a deterrent. Not too hilly, and preferably with sheds or barns that we could redo easily. Dog refuges burn money, pal. Vet fees and dog food add up."

"Grass?"

Ramon winked. "I didn't take you for a romantic, man. Of course, grass. Trees, wildflowers, fresh air."

"A rabbit or two to chase?" he joked.

"Now you're talking."

Their stroll through the warehouses had brought them to the final row. "Heartbreak Row," he murmured.

"Excuse me?" said Ramon.

"The last row...I thought this was the one called Heartbreak Row?"

"Well, that's more of a nickname. It's not the sort of term we'd use in the general public. I'm curious how you know about it."

"My friend, Katie—she's how I know about this place— she's been working with a dog here, called Prince. She used the term."

"You are friends with Katie Shields?"

Heck, he hoped so. "Er, yeah."

"She is a *legend* out here."

He grinned. "Ramon, she's a legend out there, too. In my eyes, anyway."

"Oho. Like that, is it?"

Whoa. This was not how he'd planned on declaring his heart to Katie—via gossip to a third-party intermediary who looked like a pro wrestler. "It's not...I mean, I'm not. Shoot. We might be. I'd *like* to be...man, it's complicated. Can we leave it at that?"

Ramon clapped him on the shoulder so joyfully he nearly pitched forward into the sheet-metal shed that was Heartbreak Row. "You have made my day, my friend. Want to meet Prince while you're here?"

"Yeah, sure."

"Step this way."

He followed Ramon into the dimly lit interior of the last shed. In a pen, curled up in a ball, lay a black ball of fur.

"Prince, my man. We've got company."

Prince lifted his head and his tail made a thwack-thwack-thwack noise on the floor.

Ramon lifted the latch on the gate, and the dog rolled to his feet and barreled over.

"Hey there, buddy," Anton said, as a warm, wet snout thrust itself into the palm of his hand.

"We're hoping to foster him now. Katie and Rose have worked their magic, and he's passed three park tests without lunging at other dogs. With the right owner, Prince could live a long and happy life."

"He's gorgeous."

Ramon was kneeling in the dirt beside him. "You a dog lover, man?"

"Sure."

"No, I mean are you *really* a dog lover. Because there's plenty of people out there who think they are when a dog's all cute-and-fluff, but the minute it turns out their pup's not going to be a social media sensation, they abandon it at a refuge like ours."

"That is terrible."

"Uh huh. You know what else is terrible?"

Anton eyed the giant kneeling beside him in the dust. As intuitions went, his was pretty darned healthy, and it was currently flashing on high alert. Ramon was in full promotional mode now. "What?"

"Prince here. We don't have a foster home for him. We've tried the usual channels: word of mouth, the local paper, our Reel Life account."

"Oh, man. I don't think..." Anton paused. What didn't he think? He didn't travel much anymore...like, never. He had a fully fenced garden. There was a ton of room under the desk in his study for a dog to hang out while he bashed away on his keyboard.

"Huh," he said. "Reckon he can keep up if I take him out running?"

Ramon smiled. "Why don't you try him and see? Take him for a few days, visit everywhere you might usually go with a dog, see how he copes."

Wow. This was really happening. He'd lost his heart to a girl and somehow become a foster doggy-dad along the way. "I don't have any dog food."

Ramon gave him a look that reminded him of his middle grade teacher's look when he said he'd forgotten his homework. The get-your-act-together look. "That's what pet stores are for, man. He'll need a bed, water, good quality kibble, and a harness. And love. Dogs need love, you up for that?"

Anton pulled one of Prince's ears through his fingers, and the dog's eyes went all closed and dreamy looking. "Yeah," he said. "I'm up for that."

# CHAPTER 23

*K*atie's phone buzzed just as she was finishing a mug of green tea in the break room at the control tower.

"Katie? It's me."

"Vee. Hi."

"Sorry I didn't call you last night. It was late by the time I got back, and Pete had dinner waiting, then today, work was a madhouse."

"It's fine."

"You sure? Only...there's an email from my old boss in Redwood Cove on my work computer when I logged in this morning. Says you were worried about me."

"Worried? Why would I be? I had your letter." Okay, that was a heck of a lie, and if she was a wooden toy from a fairy tale, her nose would have just skewered the refrigerator two feet in front of her.

"Umm, that's what I wanted to talk about."

No, nope, nuh uh. She was not ready to have a heart-to-heart with her sister about why she had gone into full panic stations. "Oh, heck."

"What? Why?"

Oh, double heck, had she said that out loud? She had to get off this phone call and call the Maple Ridge Police Department. She'd tried to list Veronica as a missing person! She had to make sure they didn't act on her crazy request.

"Nothing...er, listen, Vee. I'm at work, and my break's over. I've got a plane coming in. Gotta go."

"Call me, okay?"

"Sure," she said, hitting the end button. She really did have a plane coming, but for once, air traffic was going to have to manage with its star controller turning up two minutes late from break. She had a police department to call and apologize to.

A minute later, she was back at her desk, microphone in hand. *Panclan 3407, this is Redwood Cove Tower, when you're three miles from the coast marker, turn left heading T six zero maintain height approach runway two-three.*

*Redwood Cove Tower, we've got a visual on the marker.*

*Panclan 3407, it's going to be a delay, I'm going bring you back around, expect a short hold over the marker. We got a Dash-8 having problems with the localizer, we're taking a moment to get them sorted.*

*Understood. Looking to get our wheels down before the sun goes.*

*Panclan 3704, yes sir, understood, maintain your hold.*

Katie rolled her shoulders in her chair as she watched the Dash-8 line up for its landing. She waited until it was clear before she gave the go-ahead. *Panclan 3407, Redwood Cove tower here, winds are 260 at 14, you're cleared to land.*

She watched the cheerfully painted Cessna cruise in from

its holding pattern above the coast marker, then drop a wing as it found its approach angle. Daisy yellow. Perhaps she should paint her nails that color. She could do with cheering up, especially after that phone call from Vee.

She, Katie Shields, was a world class worrier. No wonder even her older sister had started avoiding her.

She dragged her thoughts away from the big mound of self-reflection she knew she needed to engage in and back to the airplane barreling along runway two-three. Another safe landing. Another happy ending. She logged the time and details on her screen, then pulled the heavy earphones away from her head. That was the final plane for the day, Redwood Cove airport was now officially shut for the night.

"All done, Katie, love?"

Andy had his keys in his hand already. Ready to get home to his pot roast, his pecan pie, and his cuddlesome wife, no doubt.

"All done, Andy."

"I'll walk you to your car."

She swallowed. "That's sweet of you to offer." Darn it, six kind words, and she could feel a sting of tears welling up. She had to do something about the way she was feeling. About the *who* she was having feelings for.

"I'm going to take a few minutes on the observation deck," she said after a moment. "Unwind a little. You okay with me locking up?"

He nodded. "Sure. You head on out."

The heavy doors to the outdoor deck squeaked as she pushed through. The breeze had some chill in it, and rain was coming, too, she was sure of it. There was a barometer in Andy's office, an old-fashioned one that would have looked more at home on a nineteenth-century sailing ship than above a high-tech bank of computer equipment. She could picture its wide brass arrow swinging around from *fair* to *change*.

If only she had an arrow that swung so easily.

The door squeaked behind her, and she looked up to see Andy, a beer in each hand. She frowned at him. "Shouldn't you be on your way home to Carmelita?"

"She's got a late shift at the hospital. Besides, if she knew I'd left my best employee moping alone on the top of this tower like Rapunzel, I'd be toast."

He handed her a beer, and she lifted it to her lips, felt the bitter ale take away a bit of the day's sting. "Man, that's good."

He grinned. "Rapunzel likes beer, who woulda thought?"

She clinked her bottle to his. "Thanks."

He took another swig, then turned to the view spread out before them. The airport's security lights twinkled, and the terminal was still lit as the last of the passengers collected their bags and found their way outside to taxis, loved ones, buses.

"You okay, Katie? Seems like you've been a little up and down lately. You were sad, then you were happy a few days back, and now you're all quiet and down again."

Andy was the sweetest guy alive, but he was still her boss, which made him the last person she'd be opening her heart up to. "I'm fine, really."

"Fine doesn't get weepy when an old man offers to walk her to her car."

She shrugged a shoulder. "I can't talk about it, Andy. I'm sorry. It's... I'm a bit...well, shoot." Now she had to go home to a much-needed bout of self-reflection *and* a cryfest. Her life sucked.

He stood there next to her, shoulder to shoulder, ignoring her valiant attempts to stay the flood of tears. "Pretty ain't she, this town of ours."

"She sure is."

"I never wanted to leave. My Carmelita, she would have lit out for L.A. or San Francisco in a heartbeat when we were young, but she stayed here for me. Busy is good and fine for those that like it. Me? I like the peaceful life."

"Me too, Andy."

He turned to her then. "You sure? Because you don't seem like you're liking anything much of late. I get it," he said when she started to speak. "You don't want to tell me what's wrong. That's your business, and I respect that. But maybe it's time you started telling *yourself* what's wrong. Because until you know, you can't fix it."

She'd barely made it in the front door from her long Monday shift, Rose capering around her like an overgrown pup, when her phone rang.

"Ramon?" she said. "What's up?"

"Good news."

"Fantastic. I need some good news. What is it?"

"Prince was picked up by a foster carer yesterday. He's not back yet, so I'm getting a good feeling. All goes well, could turn out to be a permanent placement."

"Oh, wow, that is amazing! Did you hear that, Rose?" she said, resting her hand on her dog's head. Finally, something was going right. "Your protégé is getting a second chance!"

She turned her attention back to Ramon. "Did you check

out the foster carer's premises? Who were they? Do they understand that Prince needs to be on the lead out in public?"

Ramon snorted. "Girl, you think this is my first rodeo? I've had the talk with the new owner about the lead thing. Only thing left to do is inspect the premises, but I thought I'd leave you to do that, seeing as how the new foster carer came here on your recommendation."

"On my recom—" Who on earth?

"Big guy, looks like a Hollywood stuntman. Drives a black Jeep so fine I mighta wept a little when I saw Prince sitting up there on the front seat being driven out."

Katie took a breath. How many big Hollywood-looking guys did she know, for heaven's sake, besides Ramon?

Just the one.

"Anton?" she said weakly.

"Uh huh. Anton. And girl, he is getting the Ramon seal of approval. Get on over there first chance you get and check out that man's...um, premises."

Man. She was starting to lose count of the ways she had messed up. If only she knew how to make any of it right.

# CHAPTER 24

*I*t took Anton about an hour to work out that Prince was more than a thirty-pound bundle of cute black fluff.

The first clue came at the pet store, when he discovered his new dog had a sharp and high-pitched dislike to being left alone on the front seat of a convertible Jeep.

The next day, Monday, brought new lessons for him to learn: don't leave his favorite sneakers at the bottom of the stairs, don't leave the door to his bedroom ajar unless he wanted to spend a fun few hours repacking feathers into his pillows.

The real blow—the blow that almost had him on the internet searching, by fair means or foul, for Ramon's mobile number—was the discovery of his vintage *Mother Jones Cookbook* on the floor, the recipes H through V shredded into confetti across his hand-knotted rug.

"What in blazes am I to do with you?" he asked a very happy Prince. "Two days. *Two!* I shudder to think what havoc you could wreak in a week."

The dog flopped to the floor, rested his muzzle on Anton's foot, and sighed happily.

"How are you going to become house trained, I wonder? Didn't think of that when I roared out of that refuge like a knight in shining armor, did I?"

Prince let a delicate burp escape his lips.

Anton chuckled. "Yeah. No way are you sleeping in my room tonight, pal. It's the laundry room for you. If that burp is the precursor to anything more colorful, you are going into the smallest room with the easiest to clean floor."

LATER, he struggled to fall asleep. The first reason was a good one: his manuscript had just passed the thirty-thousand word mark, and thoughts on how to rescue his criminal mastermind from the snake-infested jungle he'd just parachuted down into to escape a British assassin on a dilapidated cargo plane were too fun to sleep through.

The other reasons? Katie, of course. She'd not turned up to collect the agony aunt letter he'd found, and he hadn't yet apologized for laughing at her. He'd spent hours regretting allowing Danny and Jules to coax him into taking over that column on *Page Seventeen*.

The other reason was almost as worrisome. Two howls from the laundry room just before midnight had his blood curdling before he remembered he had a new house guest, and he struggled to settle after that, wondering if Prince was going to howl for hours. The dog didn't make another peep, but when the familiarly irritating buzz of his alarm sounded at six a.m., Anton felt like he'd only just closed his eyes.

"Man," he said to the empty room. "What idiot set that alarm clock?"

Oh, right. Him.

He rolled out of bed. Time to find out if Ramon had been joking when he said Prince would be up for a five-mile run.

Downstairs, he opened the laundry room door, expecting to see a re-imagining of the apocalypse, and was flummoxed to see a sleepy dog sitting up on the plush bed he'd been bought, a white tiled floor empty of accidents. No scratched doors, no carnage, no shredded clothes pins or laundry baskets or anything.

"Prince," he said. "My man! Good job!"

The dog took the opportunity of an open door to dart past and head for the garden, where he spent a long and apparently happy minute lifting his leg against the hydrangeas.

"Fancy a jog, Prince?"

Woof.

And a few minutes later there was a mile under their belt, and man and dog were flying along the track to the beach.

Maybe he didn't need to search for Ramon's mobile number quite yet.

A BATTERED green hatchback was parked in his driveway when he and the dog huffed their way up the last quarter mile from town.

Two sets of eyes turned to face him from through its windows. Brown ones—Rose—happy as could be. And greenish ones—Katie's—with an expression he couldn't read.

Let it be happy, he thought. Happy, like he was to see her.

He jogged to a standstill and rested a sweaty palm on the roof of her car, ignoring the capering madness of Prince, who had spotted Rose and was attempting to leap in through a car window to join her.

"Katie," he said. "You're just in time for waffles."

She looked pale, and there were shadows beneath her eyes that he'd have brushed away if he could.

"I'm here on refuge business," she said.

Huh. So, all, whatever *all* was, was not forgotten.

"About that," he said. "I'm a little worried about my new refuge dog, Prince. He doesn't seem quite..."

"Quite what?" she said, looking concerned and pushing the car door open, resulting in a stampede of furry feet as Prince tried to rocket into the hatchback just as Rose tried to rocket out.

"Dogs!" she said sharply as she fought her way through the chaos. "Sit."

A second later, two statue-like beasts were seated before her, looking as though they were ready to compete in an obedience show. She held out a hand, which the dogs must have interpreted as *stay*, because they both remained frozen even when she moved a few steps from the car. His Katie had skills.

"He looks settled, that's a good sign. What's worrying you?"

He had his leverage, and now he was going to use it. "It'd be easier to show you inside than to explain."

"Hmm," she sniffed.

"Over waffles."

"I'm not here for breakfast, Anton."

He tried for a mournful look. It had certainly worked for

his new house guest the night before, when he was standing over the ruins of a once-unchewed cookbook. "For Prince," he said, adding a heavy sigh.

Her eyes narrowed. "I guess Rose and I have a bit of time. For Prince."

He followed her into the house, then dropped a wink to his new dog. "Sausages. Tonight, on the grill, buddy. My treat."

AN HOUR LATER, Katie was on her third waffle, and she seemed to have forgotten she was here to talk about his fictitious Prince problems. He rested a hand on the remnants of his now-battered copy of *Mother Jones Cookbook*. Perhaps the unexpected jump to W was working in his favor.

"Another?" he said, the jug of batter poised in his hand.

"I couldn't. Wow. I didn't know I was hungry until I tried the first one, and then when I tried it? Those blueberries, were they dusted in—"

"Confectioner's sugar, yep."

"And the batter! There was something, I just can't—"

He grinned. "Vanilla bean extract. Homemade. I know, I've got skills."

She was grinning up at him, and he almost forgot his worry about how he was going to break the news of the Agony Aunt letter to her.

Almost, but not quite. "Coffee on the patio?" he said.

"Sure. But listen, you cooked, I should wash up."

"It's fine. I've got all day to clean up. I'll bring the pot out. There's…er, something I need to show you."

"On Prince? Does he have a hotspot? Fluffy dogs can be prone to them."

"No, not at all."

She walked to the sink and rinsed her plate and cutlery off before piling them neatly on the drain board.

There was no way this was going to end well.

# CHAPTER 25

*K*atie dried her plate and rested it in the rack. She'd come out here prepared to be all aloof and businesslike. Check that the premises met the requirements of the refuge, show Anton Thriller Price that she didn't care a hoot about him or his dumb prowess with silly word games, and then get the heck back into her hatchback and zoom off into an amazing future.

She hadn't expected to be charmed.

Waffles…who could be served homemade waffles made by a good-looking guy in a polka-dot apron poring over the chewed-up remains of a 1960s family cookbook and *not* feel their resolve soften? And if he thought she hadn't noticed the scraps of cooked batter he'd slipped to the adoring dogs at his feet, he was mistaken.

Anton Price may be annoyingly good at word games and a little insensitive about her own cloddish ineptness at them, but he was a sweetheart. No one could resist that.

No one whose name began with Katie and ended with Shields, anyway.

"I've been pretty upset with you for a few days," she confessed.

He winced. "I know. About that—"

"You don't have to explain."

"I want to. Because...that's not all I have to explain."

"You look serious," she said. He also looked wary.

This was not good. Maybe she should just find her keys and make her excuses. She'd found Veronica, after all, and that was the only thing that had connected her and Anton. Prince had found a home. That was all her responsibilities taken care of, wasn't it? If she could just teach Rose not to dig holes under the hydrangea, she could kid herself she'd had a win-win month, and not admit what a giant emotional mess it had actually been.

"I wasn't meaning to make fun of you the other day."

Oh, she did not want to get into this. She'd overreacted about her sister going on a week-long trip with her new friend. She'd overreacted to that comment of Anton's. She was a lousy judge of what was going on around her, and her emotions were shot.

"You don't have to apologize," she said. "It was probably me, getting it wrong. I seem to be doing that a lot lately."

"I don't think less of people who aren't into word games like I am. I am clueless about loads of things, dog training for one," he said, spreading his arms to encompass the dog toy massacre that must have occurred sometime during the brief period Prince had been resident in the house.

"I've spent a year teaching myself to cook because when I turned thirty, I couldn't boil an egg," he went on. "I failed my driving test three times, I have a tantrum when I can't find my car keys, and I fall asleep when anyone tries to talk to me about politics."

Every last failure just made him more of a sweetheart. And made her more of an ogre for overreacting. Why was she finding it so hard to find the words to admit she had stuff going on in her head which she wasn't handling very well?

"That's not all, Katie. I've found something. A letter in the *Dear Anna* section. I think it's the one you're looking for."

Darn it. Now she'd messed up again. She hadn't even told Anton that she'd been in contact with Veronica. He'd been sweet enough to come with her on a stakeout, call in a favor with his bank manager, dig through dusty back issues of newsprint for her, and she'd not even thanked him, or let him know the crisis was over.

Self-absorbed, that's what she was.

"Anton. I've spoken to Veronica."

"You have? Katie, that's great!" He was swinging her in a hug before she knew what was what. How she wished she could stay there, held, warm, cared for.

She pushed herself away. "Turns out, I wasted your time."

"No, Katie, I—"

"She wasn't abducted by aliens or held against her will by some doomsday conspiracy theorist."

"That's...good news, isn't it? Why are you sounding disappointed?"

Shoot, did she? She sighed. "I'm disappointed with myself, to be honest."

"For what? Being concerned about your closest living relative? That doesn't make you a disappointment, it makes you a great sister."

"What? No, that's—"

She broke off. He didn't know the worst of it. Sure, she'd overreacted. She had been worried, but had she been worried that Vee was in trouble? Or had she been worried about what she, Katie, would do without her?

Worse, her worry had banked down to a low simmer as soon as she'd started getting to know Anton. Some days, she'd been more worried about what dress to wear so he'd think she looked pretty than she had about her own older sister. What was wrong with her?

"I think," Anton said gently, his hand coming to land on hers, "that maybe you were worried about yourself. You missed her. You were lonely. You were worried how you would ever fill the void if you became less important in her life."

"That is so not true," she said, but the tears that had started streaming down her face like the Hoover dam wall had just broken were saying something totally different.

"I get it," he said. "Katie, please. Tell me what's wrong."

She wanted to snap at him, like Prince would have snapped at anything that made him anxious a few weeks ago. Fear aggression—it was a thing, right?

But in the battle between fight or flight, flight won. She wasn't ready to admit anything to Anton. Even more, she wasn't ready to admit anything to herself.

"I have to go."

"Katie, please. You're upset. Maybe I should drive you?"

"No. Thank you, I just..." Darn it, where had she dropped her purse?

"Before you go. I know this is a bad time, but—there's something else." He lifted a sealed plastic bag from the counter. In it was a sky-blue envelope. "I told you I found a letter which I think might have been the clue you needed. This is the original that came to the newspaper office."

Her sister's trademark stationery; she'd know it anywhere. Grabbing it from him, she picked up her purse from where she'd spied it on a stool below the counter and motioned a downcast Rose to her side.

"If you want to talk about this, you know where I am," he said. "Anytime, Katie. I mean that."

She couldn't speak, so she got the heck out.

# CHAPTER 26

"I've got some chores to do, pal," said Anton to the dog at his feet. "Can you be trusted not to destroy my garden if I leave you home alone for an hour?"

Prince gave a yawn and rolled over onto his back. A week he'd lived at the cottage, and now he thought he was king.

"I'll take that as a yes." With a bit of luck, the hell-hound he was now responsible for would be too worn out from his morning run to chew up anything else.

He pulled his satchel over his shoulder. The day was too glorious to drive, and the *Cove to Coast Herald* office was only a ten-minute stroll down the cliff track. He'd walk.

And think.

Like he'd been thinking ever since Katie had hurried away from his house in her ancient hatchback.

He'd wanted her to stay as much as he'd wanted to keep breathing. He needed to tell her that...to let her know that she wasn't the only one who struggled sometimes to work out how much to care, how much to let go.

How much to live.

She'd taught him that. Or rather, the feeling in his heart that had been growing bit by bit since he'd first met her had taught him that. He was tired of living quietly in his cliffside house, living a half-life.

He wanted more. Heck, he wanted it all. And his all started with a prickly, warm-hearted, soft-skinned woman called Katie.

But he had to get his own house in order first, and for that he needed to talk to Danny.

THE NEWSPAPER OFFICE was full of hammering and muttered oaths when he arrived.

He walked through the foyer and into the back office, to where a huge man in overalls was frowning down into an open toolbox. Julie sat at the desk where she paid the bills. "What's going on?"

"Safe cracker," she said.

"I thought we found the code two weeks ago? In Danny's diary."

"Oh, we did, pet. Worked a treat."

He looked over to the corner of the room, where Danny was kneeling on the floor beside the green-enameled safe. "I don't understand. Danny?"

"Oh, don't disturb him, Anton. He's thinking."

He raised his eyebrows at her.

"He decided to use a new code when he locked it last night. Now he can't remember what he chose, so Trevor here," she nodded at the overalls guy, "is seeing what he can do."

"Might be an explosives job, Danny," said Trevor.

"Son of a gun. That safe is older than I am. It's precious, Trev."

"It's also stubborn as an old mule."

"You got a minute, Danny?" Anton said.

"Maybe. If it comes with a cup of coffee and a cookie, I do."

Anton raised his eyebrows helplessly at Jules.

She nodded. "Cookies in the tin," she mouthed.

He headed for the kitchen nook, found a fresh batch of something chunky and home-made in the tin as promised, and checked the coffee pot.

Danny took his coffee black, which was lucky, because the milk in the fridge smelled like something a dumpster would refuse to accept. He tipped its remains down the sink and filled Danny's favorite mug.

"Here," he said, carrying his peace offering back out to the workroom. "Now can we talk? It's about *Page Seventeen*."

"Love it. Keep up the good work," said Danny. "Getting a lot of great feedback about those photos you put in."

"Er...thanks. Here's the thing. I'm working on a manuscript that's going to take up a lot of my time."

Danny stopped rifling through the real estate pages at the back of an old issue of the paper. "You're not quitting!"

"This was always a temporary gig, Danny."

"I don't accept your resignation. As your boss, I insist you continue."

He snorted. "Danny, you don't even pay me. I do this for fun, remember?"

"We can pay. Julia? Julia? Find the checkbook would you, my love. Mr. Price here is extorting money from an old man."

"We don't need the checkbook, Jules," he said. "It's not the money. I don't need money, I need time."

"But the readers, Anton. They love your column. I've got local advertisements lined up for months wanting to get on *Page Seventeen.*"

He held his hands up in the air. "No can do, old friend."

"Don't you *old friend* me. Sucking the lifeblood out of my newspaper like this, you oughta be ashamed. After I took you in outa the goodness of my heart."

He chuckled. "You came to me, Danny. Well, to be fair, it was Jules who delivered your message."

Danny was on a roll. All that was missing was a stage and a spotlight. "I took you in when no one else would give you a job in this town."

"You don't pay me; I thought we'd covered that."

"The perfidy of young people. Spineless shifters. Wasteful whippersnappers. No respect, none, my father started this business in 1926 and he's spinning in his grave today, young man. Spinning."

Anton struggled to hide his grin. Jules had been right. Danny *was* easy to manage, you just had to know how. "Of course, if we could simplify my page down a bit. Make it less...burdensome."

Danny narrowed his eyes. "Now, see? That's more like it. What's your best offer?"

"I do the crosswords, that's all."

"Nope, no way, not happening," said Danny, the light of battle in his eye. "The Agony Aunt column has been a feature in this paper since my granddaddy was in knickerbockers, and it's staying."

"I thought your father started this business. You know, the one who's spinning in his grave."

"Don't use your word tricks on me, young man. The letters

column has to stay."

"Gee, that's a shame. Give my farewells in the next issue, won't you?" He took a long stride to the door.

"Now, son. There's no call to be hasty."

He waited.

Danny harrumphed. "This is my final offer, and if you don't take it you'll be back on the streets. The crossword and the photo column. It's that or nothing."

Anton could see Jules standing in the doorway, bearing witness to the spectacle.

"You drive a hard bargain, Danny," he said, lowering his voice an octave and offering his hand for the old man to shake. If he'd known how easy it was going to be to ditch that pesky *Dear Anna* column from *Page Seventeen*, he'd have tried this months ago.

"Darn straight I do," Danny said.

Anton dropped Jules a wink and clapped Danny around the shoulder. He loved his gig here at the newspaper, and now he could keep it with a clear conscience.

He stood in the doorway of the *Cove to Coast Herald* for a moment, checking out the buzz of tourists milling their way along the historic district while he planned out the rest of his day.

Land. That was next on his list. His eye fell on the newsstand by the door, where today's issue of the paper lay in a neat pile for passers-by. Perfect. He slipped a few coins in the slot and helped himself to one. Time to see what was on offer in the back pages, where all the local real estate agents hawked their listings.

He needed a takeout coffee. A picnic bench in the sun. And five shady acres of land.

# CHAPTER 27

*K*atie sat on the timber step that led from the back porch to the garden. Late afternoon sunlight was dancing through the leaves of the old orange tree, and she turned her face into the warmth.

It wasn't cold, not really...but the sun was a comfort. Something about all that bright yellow never failed to cheer her.

She sighed when she heard the noise of a car pulling into the front of the house and looked again at the blue envelope in her hand. She had struggled to find the courage to read her sister's Agony Aunt letter, which had meant a long week of procrastination. And now her sister had arrived, in person, and ignoring her problems was no longer an option.

Beside her, Rose lifted her heavy head, her ears pricked.

"Yes," she said. "It's Vee. Go let her in, Rose." The big dog gave a woof, then bolted in through the house to the front door. Katie stayed where she was and listened to the excited clicks of her dog's nails on the floorboards, then the measured tread of her sister's shoes as she came down the hall.

"Katie?"

"I'm out back," she said, and wiped her clammy palms on the rough denim of her jeans. "Come on in."

"Hey, sis!" Her sister pushed open the old screen door and let it slam back into the house with a bang, like she always had, ever since she was little. Veronica traveled everywhere with her own little hurricane of energy spinning about her, all noise and lipstick and drama.

The cloud of smell came first: perfume, a waft of coffee, and a heady reek of turpentine that let her know Vee had spent part of the day on one of her DIY projects. Next was the hug.

"How are you? Gosh, it's been weeks since I saw you last," said Veronica, letting her go after a final squeeze and settling on the timber step beside her. "Yes, okay, I've missed you too," she said to Rose, batting her away. "Go find a plant to destroy, would you?"

Katie sniffed. A dog person, her sister was not.

Her sister seemed to have worked out she was the only one saying anything. "Katie? You okay?"

She took a breath and handed over the blue envelope.

"What's this? One of my letters?"

"Read it."

"I don't understa—"

The silence was enough to tell her that Veronica had just read the front. The envelope wasn't addressed to Katie Shields, 47 Prospect Street. It was addressed to Anna Tugoy.

"How did you get this?"

She blew out a breath. "How did I get this? Not from you, Veronica. So come on, I'm all ears, what does it say?"

Her sister sighed. "Katie. I don't even remember what I wrote, to be honest. It was a long time ago."

"I'm waiting."

She had to wait a good while longer, as her sister took her time unfolding the flap of the envelope and pulling out the paper folded within. *"Dear Anna,"* her sister said aloud.

"Anna's a guy, by the way," she couldn't help saying, in a snarky tone she hadn't used since she was about fourteen. Turns out, finding out her sister would rather blab about her private business in a public newspaper column than talk to her made her feel snarky.

Veronica cleared her throat. *"I've got a problem, and it's been festering in my head and making me unhappy, so I thought I would write for advice. Here's the thing. I met someone, and I'm pretty sure this guy is the one, not just some foolish crush (that's a whole other story!). Problem is, I'm worried how my getting involved with some-one, really involved, will affect my sister."*

Katie pressed her fingers to her eyes. Was she so much of a burden?

Her sister hesitated, then carried on reading aloud. *"The man that raised us passed away a year ago, and we've been really close ever since. I moved away recently for work, and my sister got really sad and quiet. Now if I start making time for someone else in my life, will that make her even more sad?"*

Katie was crying now, and for some dumb reason, her shoulders and lungs had decided to join in the party and turn her tears into a full-blown sob-fest. But also crying, she real-ized with a shock, was her sister.

*"If I had to choose,"* Veronica continued, her voice thick. *"I'd choose her. But Anna...I really don't want to have to choose."*

The only sound for a long moment was the ka-kaw-ka of a

quail from somewhere in the neighboring garden. Katie felt the sun on her face while she listened to her sister's sad sniffles beside her. This was the moment when she needed to step up, move away from her fear of being left alone and lonely. If only it didn't feel so hard.

She let out a long breath, then began. "Vee?"

"Yes, honey."

"I wanted to be mad at you and make this all your fault but really...I think I've been a big idiot."

Her sister's tears dissolved into a snort. "Of course you have. You're a Shields, aren't you? When we do anything, we do it like rock stars. Idiocy included."

She tried to say more, but her sister wrapped her in a hug so tight words became impossible. Eventually, she had to fight her way out of the stranglehold in order to take a breath.

"Cup of tea?" she said. "Followed by a long overdue talk?"

"I thought you'd never ask. Come on, let's sit in the kitchen."

They slipped into an old routine, Vee filling the kettle while Katie pulled mugs from the hooks on the old cabinet.

"So," Veronica said, once they were seated across from each other at the scarred Formica table. "Confession time. Okay, I've been worried about you, but I've also been having some relationship dramas, and I've been frazzled. I wrote that letter just after I moved out to Maple Ridge. It was a dumb move. I should have just talked to you, but I was...scared. A bit selfish too, if I'm being honest. I'd just met Pete, and I wanted to just think about me for a while. I'm sorry, Katie."

Katie took a sip of the green tea she'd brewed. "Okay. Confession time for me, too. I didn't hear from you for a few days, and you weren't returning my calls. Then I misplaced your next letter—it slid under the sofa, and I didn't find it for a week—and yeah, I kinda went nuts."

"How nuts are we talking?"

"Oh, it's up there. I reported you missing at the Maple Ridge Police Department."

Veronica was halfway through a cookie, and a spray of crumbs hit the table as she gasped. "You what?"

She shrugged. "Idiot, remember?"

Her sister's lips twitched, then her nose, then she let out a whoop that would have silenced every quail in a ten-mile radius. "The police department," she snickered. "Oh, that's good. That is so funny."

She couldn't help it; her sister's laugh was so infectious. "I marched on in there snapping my fingers. They cowered before me."

The snort her sister made would have done a pig proud. "You did not. Stop it."

"I left no stone unturned. Your current boss. Your ex-boss. Your ornery eighty-three-year-old neighbor. Even..." oh boy, this really was confession time. She winced. "I even tried to find out who the guy was at your old job that you had a crush on."

"*Freeman?* But that was like, a year ago...and he barely knew who I was."

"Well," she sniffed. "He knows who you are now."

"Wow."

Yeah. Wow. As her sister's laugh dried up, she held her hand out across the table. "I can see that it's all ridiculous. I know why it's funny. But the real confession is this, Vee: I really didn't think it was funny or ridiculous at the time."

"You want to tell me about it?"

She had to tell someone, and who better then Vee, who knew her better than she knew herself?

"I've been stressed. About a lot of things, over such a long time. I've just kept it all bottled up instead of talking it out, and when I couldn't get hold of you, I wasn't able to think rationally about it."

"Ok. When did all the stress start?"

"Uncle Roly's funeral. It was a sunny day, do you remember? And we'd plucked every flower from the garden here to make a wreath for his service. The grass was so green, the sky was so blue, the sun so high in the sky...but I couldn't feel any of it. I just felt cold. All day, and almost every day since, until—"

No. She wasn't going to think about Anton. Not yet. He came later.

"Maybe we should have seen a counselor, both of us," said Veronica.

"Yeah. But then, of course, the state was in lockdown, and we all had to deal with those months of uncertainty. Then I met Jetson."

"Jetson the rat."

She smiled. "He wasn't that bad, was he?"

"He never loved you."

"Well, to be fair, I never loved him. But still, it stung when he took off as though I'd meant nothing at all."

Vee nodded. "And then I left you."

Katie took in a breath. "I needed to let you go, but I wasn't ready. I think, after Uncle Roly died, I had this idea that you were now the head of the family, and would look out for me like he always did."

"I *will* look out for you, Katie."

"Yeah. I know. But we're both adults. It's time I started living like one."

"You're being too hard on yourself. You have a fabulous job, you volunteer at the refuge. That's about as adult as it gets, Katie."

Perhaps. But it wasn't enough. "I've had an idea, but I'm not sure if you'll like it."

Veronica raised her eyebrows. "Try me."

"This house. I'd like to buy you out of your half. It's time I started thinking of it as my house, not Uncle Roly's house."

"Oh!"

"Think about it. You could use the money to put into your house-flipping business. And I could stop living my life as though I'm in a holding pattern. I need to land, Vee. I need to feel some solid ground beneath my feet."

Vee had tears in her eyes as she looked around the faded blue paint on the kitchen cupboards, the door to the laundry room where their heights at various ages had been carefully etched. "I love this place, Katie. But I've been ready to move on from it for a long time. I'd be pleased to sell you my half."

"You would?"

"Of course I would, you nut. I just hope home ownership really will help you feel...grounded."

Katie hid a grin. "It was Tuna Yango who gave me the idea."

"It was *who?* Oh, you mean the crossword compiler? How on earth—?"

"Um, yeah. This is the part of the missing-person crisis I didn't tell you yet."

"I am agog. Start talking."

"His name is Anton."

Her sister held both her hands up in the air like she was bringing in a jumbo jet to land. "Wait, wait...is that a blush I see on your cheeks? Oh my word, that is a blush. You met a guy while hunting me down?"

"Yeah. I met a guy." She smiled, and a few tears may have slipped down her cheeks, but they were happy and hopeful ones this time, not desperate ones.

"Well, come on over here and give me a hug, so I can cry again, too."

She slid her arms around her sister and buried her face in her neck. "Love you, Vee."

"Love you too, Katie. Now." Vee said, pulling her face away. "Forget the tea pot; is there wine somewhere in this ancient fridge I no longer own half of?"

"Sure."

"I'll pour, you talk. Tell me *everything*."

# CHAPTER 28

The park in the center of Maple Ridge was busy on Friday lunchtime. Anton realized, as he looked across at Prince sitting high and mighty in the front seat of his Jeep, that he may not have thought this through.

First problem: he had to walk into a bank to persuade a woman he'd never met that he needed to talk to her. Second problem: he had a dog on probation who couldn't be left alone tied up at the bank's door.

Where there was a will, there was a way, he thought. And he had one heck of a will.

"Prince, old friend. Today is important, okay?"

A terrier with mismatched brown and white ears was flying across the park's grass in pursuit of a ball, and Prince had never seemed less interested in anything he had to say. He was straining at his car harness and had started to drool, his eyes fixed on the running dog.

"We don't drool on leather, pal," he said. "And we play nice. Understood?"

Prince gave a woof as Anton unclicked him from the seat belt, but didn't lunge for freedom, which was a good sign.

He hoped.

The bank turned out to be dog friendly, which definitely was a good sign. He was about to ask a teller if she could let Veronica Shields know she had a visitor, when a tall woman with a direct green gaze that had to be from the same gene pool as Katie's walked past him.

"Vee?" he said.

She came to an abrupt stop beside him. "Excuse me?"

"You must be Vee. You have Katie's eyes."

Those green eyes widened. "Holy mackerel. You must be the guy."

Hmm. It was hard to read whether that was a good thing or a bad thing.

She dropped her eyes to the black furry beast at his feet. "And Prince. Wow. Just ... wow."

"Can we talk? Do you have a minute?"

She had her hand under his arm and was guiding him out of the bank in the space of a heartbeat. "For you, Anton, I have my whole lunch hour. You can buy me and Prince a hotdog in the park and then ..."

Okay. So she hadn't hated him at first sight, which was the best sign yet. Katie must have said *something* nice about him at least for her sister to be willing to talk. "And then?"

Her grin was fast and such an exact match for Katie's, it made his head spin.

"Then, you can tell me *everything*."

～

HE WAS PRETTY sure *everything* didn't include the kiss on the front porch. Holding Katie's hand as they walked the quiet streets of Redwood Cove. Especially not feeling his heart tear a little as Katie cried over the agony aunt letter in the little blue envelope.

He could spin out a story into a hundred-thousand-word blockbuster when the mood took him, but today wasn't about some long-winded narrative about how he'd come to know Katie, and how she made him feel, and the conflicts along the way that had somehow brought them closer together.

Today was just about the emotion.

"I'm in love with your sister," he said.

"Oh, Anton." Veronica looked at him across the picnic table, a sauce-stained napkin forgotten in her hand. "Have you told Katie that?"

He swallowed. "That's been a little tricky. Last time I saw her, she was running out of my house crying."

"Yeah. There's been a bit of that lately from us Shields girls."

"Have you seen her?"

"Yeah. We caught up."

"She was pretty worried about you."

"I know, she told me. The stakeout on my apartment, the police department."

"Where were you? Oh...sorry. You don't have to answer that. Curiosity is one of my bad habits."

She grinned. "I'd expect nothing less from Tuna Yango."

He shook his head. "That silly pen name."

"No way! I liked to imagine I was the only one who'd clued in that the crossword compiler and the *Dear Anna* columnists were both anagrams of Agony Aunt. I love that page. And sharing it was something Katie and I got a lot of joy out of. Well...more me than her to be honest. I thought she loved playing crossword games with me, turns out she wasn't that interested."

"Yeah. She's a one-plus-one girl, she keeps telling me."

Her sister smiled. "You know, I think I like you, Anton Price. Enough to maybe not cause a fuss that you called me Vee. I'm Veronica to most people, all four syllables."

He tilted his head. "Well, when we first got acquainted, your name was Very Secretive, wasn't it? You are the person who wrote in, I take it?"

She nodded, then began shredding the serviette into strips. "Yeah. That was me."

"I'm giving up that column."

"You are? People love *Dear Anna*."

He shrugged. "I never liked doing it. It seemed false, assuming you know enough about someone from a couple of paragraphs to give them life advice. It's a gimmick to sell newspapers, not counseling."

"Maybe. But can I tell you something, Anton? Because you look as though you've been beating yourself up over this even more than I have. If I hadn't written that letter, and you hadn't given it to Katie all these months later, she and I might never have talked out the things we needed to talk out."

He frowned. "There was some sort of circuitous logic in there that I couldn't follow."

"She reads the Saturday paper on the back step, with a mug of tea, like clockwork. When I put that letter in, I was so sure she'd see it. I needed a..."

"An ice breaker?"

Vee smiled at him. "Exactly. But then for some reason, she

didn't see it when she needed to, and I chickened out about showing her. So it's good that you gave it to her."

He felt the dog shift at his feet so that a heavy snout was tucked up against his ankle. The connection was a comfort. "I don't know about that."

"I *do* know, Anton. Trust me on this. Because of you, Katie and I have been able to work things out. Me and Katie are good. Really good, for the first time in a long time. So good, in fact, that I'm going to tell you a little secret."

He took a breath. "This isn't a *Dear Anna* thing, is it? Because I've given that up."

"This is a Katie thing."

"I'm listening."

"Yes."

"Yes?"

"I'm confused. I haven't asked you a question."

She smiled at him and rose to her feet. "Oh, Anton, of course you have. You drove all this way because you wanted to know something. And I'm telling you, the answer is yes."

He took a deep breath. "You're being very cryptic, Vee."

"I know. I have to be. Katie's an independent woman, and it's not up to me to sort out her life; she'll do a fine job all on her own. I'm just...giving you a little clue."

And with a wink, and a waggle of her fingers to the dog, she was gone.

～

YES.

One little word, and one little clue. He practiced the questions that might go with it in his head. Did Katie love him? *Yes.*

Was Vee okay with him wooing her sister? *Yes.*

"Or I've got this all totally wrong," he said to Prince as he led him back to the car past two poodles and a Chihuahua in a candy-pink dog suit, all of whom Prince nobly ignored, "and the question Vee was actually answering, was *Did you enjoy your hotdog?*"

This was too important to get wrong.

He dropped gears as he wound the Jeep back down the mountain pass. He had a ninety-minute drive back to Redwood Cove. How many cryptic clues had he worked out over the years? Created, wrapped in neat black-and-white boxes, curated?

Hundreds. Thousands.

But this was the one he needed to get right.

He looked at his watch. Vee had said Katie read the *Cove to Coast Herald* cover to cover every Saturday morning on the back step. He had a plan. A wild, hairy, audacious plan...but did he have time. He tapped the talk setting on his steering wheel that linked to his phone. "Call Jules," he commanded.

"*Cove to Coast Herald*, Julia speaking."

"Jules, it's me. I need a favor."

"What, my love?"

"I want to change my page for tomorrow's edition. What's the deadline?"

"For tomorrow?" she squeaked. "Oh, pet, it's sent."

"Can we unsend it?"

"Well, yes, if I call Reggie up at the printers. How much time do you need?"

Shoot. He had another hour's drive, and he had to visit a

store in town and drive out to the airport too. Another hour to typeset. "Can I have until four p.m.?"

"For you, pet, consider it done."

"You're a sweetheart, Jules. I don't care what Danny says about you."

She giggled, as well she might. Danny loved Julia even more than he loved his antique safe. "What's the big rush?"

"I just thought of the perfect photo for *Page Seventeen*."

His next phone call was not going to be as quick. He hit the talk button on his dash again. "Call Dr. Alice Goodly."

He had a cured patient to report.

# CHAPTER 29

Katie opened the Saturday edition of the *Cove to Coast Herald*, swiping off the little curls of shredded newspaper that Rose's canine teeth had created. She couldn't believe she was awake at—she stared at her wrist-watch blearily—five a.m.

She needed tea, possibly a whole pot of it, which was why she'd brought the old brown pot with its battered owl cozy out with her to the back step.

The sun was hours away, but the light from the open kitchen door spilled out like a small moon, giving her plenty of light to read.

Summer Festival articles, a full-page spread on the Mayor's Green-the-Streets campaign, and—deep in the middle of the paper—the page Veronica had been using for her crossword lessons every week for months.

Katie rarely bothered reading *Page Seventeen*—the cross-word clues had been a chore, not fun, and she had no interest in reading other people's personal business—she'd just kept up with it because it was important to Vee.

Today, however, she looked. She *really* looked. Anton, and the terrible way she'd run out of his house the other day, had been top of her thoughts. She had to explain, and she would...she just needed to get herself together a little first.

That process had started. Talking things out with Veronica, making the decision to purchase the other half of Uncle Roly's...*her* house.

She was feeling her two feet planted a little more firmly on the ground every day now, and soon she'd be ready to go see Anton. Maybe find out what all these feelings she had for him really meant.

Until then, *Page Seventeen* was the perfect way for her to spend a little more time getting to know him. She knew how much he loved the photos he included on the page...now she could try and work out why.

She smoothed the page out across the top step, anchoring it down with her teapot. On the top left, in a curly, old-fashioned font, sat the *Dear Anna* column and beneath it, a notice. *Anna has just announced she is retiring from the Agony Aunt business, and this will be her last column in the Cove to Coast Herald. She wishes all her letter writers the best of futures.*

Giving it up? He'd be happy about that, she hoped. Hadn't he said he'd been reluctant to take it on?

She dropped her eyes to the first letter. Some teenager named *Grossed Out 15* was having an existential crisis because their mom insisted on kissing them goodbye every morning at the school gate.

*Ouch, that's a tough one*, wrote Anna. *Two suggestions: one subtle, one hardcore. You could go on a fitness kick and tell your mom you're walking to school...or maybe just the last few blocks if you live too far away. Or, my young, brave, grossed out fifteen-year-old, if you're up to it, the truth is always a good strategy. Tell mom all that kissy-at-the-gate stuff is embarrassing you, but you still love her, and suggest a new goodbye habit instead, like a fist bump. Mom may love that, and you won't know unless you speak up. Yours, Anna Tugoy.*

Speaking up...not a relationship strategy Katie had ever mastered in the past, but one she meant to embrace in the future. Leaving the rest of the Agony Aunt column for later, she glanced over to the right-hand side crossword section.

*Fifteen across, eight letters: Let's all go in to get her,* she read. Oh! Well, for the first time ever, she could see the answer. To get her...together, meaning *all.* She looked up at the sky, expecting thunder clouds to be rolling in, a lightning strike at the very least. She, Katie, had solved a clue!

Typical. Now that she and Vee had agreed the weekly clue lesson could stop, she was finally getting the hang of these suckers.

The section that took up the bottom half of the page was the *Happy Snaps* section. She was about to flip past it and keep going through the rest of the paper, when she recognized the image.

The photo was taken with a panoramic setting and covered green patchwork fields, towering stands of cypress and oak, and the town of Redwood Cove nestled between cliff and ocean. This view...it was *her* view, from the observation deck at the control tower.

But how—?

She knew who had taken it the second she started reading the blurb. *Happy Snaps which appear here are chosen from Cove to*

*Coast Herald's Reel Life account. Upload your scenic photo and tell us why your photo makes you happy.*

*Photo by Anton Price.*

What? No anagrammed name preserving his anonymity? No jokes? No *game*?

*The place where I took this photo is important to me because this is where I have hidden a small, velvet box. In the box is a ring. On the ring is an engraving. I wasn't sure what to have engraved on the ring at first.*

*I'll let you into a secret: I have a thing for words. I like playing with them, twisting them, turning them in and out and finding all the nuances and innuendoes that like to hide within ...*

*But then I knew: the words I needed to choose were not for a game, or a puzzle, because love is not a game.*

*Love is truth and honesty and forever.*

*If you're reading this—and you know who you are—come and find your ring.*

Katie pressed a hand to her heart. Did this mean...? Was he...?

Oh boy.

"Rose?" she called.

Her golden dog trotted in from the dark of the back garden, a tendril of rose bush clinging to her whiskers.

"We've got an emergency, Rose. Help me find my car keys."

THE AIRPORT WAS STILL DARK when she pulled into the car park below the tower, the only glow coming from thin pools of gold below the streetlights. Soon the ticket agents would be arriving, the baggage handlers, the couple who ran the snacks kiosk, but for now, airplanes gleamed in the moonlight from their tidy row beside the terminal. Baggage trucks were tucked away in their sheds, mobile stairs and catering lifts were out of sight, even the windsocks dangled quietly from their poles.

If only her heart was as quiet.

It wasn't. It had galloped into a frenzy when she had read Anton's message. What if she hadn't read the paper? What if she'd missed that paragraph? What would he have done then?

She fumbled with her keys at the door to the tower. How he had wrangled his way into the restricted space of the control tower was a mystery for another day, but she bet the solution began with an A and ended with an N, D, and Y.

The elevator hummed as it sped upwards, a noise she suspected her strung-out nerves were also making in some frequency she couldn't detect. The doors slid open, she moved a step forward, three steps to the right, and there she was, at the solid security door which led to the view...and whatever else might be out there waiting for her.

Well. Now or never. She found the key on her office set, unlocked the door and stepped out.

The first thing she noticed was the breeze. It lifted her hair and carried with it the salt of the ocean, the cool of the giant sequoias guarding Griffin State Park. The second thing was the small, dark box sitting alone in the center of the neatly swept floor.

She sat cross-legged on the floor to inspect it.

She could open it here, alone, with her little patch of California spread out before her, and the dawn pushing fingers of light through her little patch of sky...but she was tired of being alone.

She picked up the box, shoved it into the pocket of her jacket and jumped to her feet.

She knew exactly where she wanted to be when she opened this box and read whatever was engraved inside. And she knew exactly who she wanted to have beside her when she did.

# CHAPTER 30

*E*very house Anton passed seemed to have a copy of the *Cove to Coast Herald* rolled up in its driveway. Old dogs woofed at him and Prince as they ran by, curtains twitched, and the smells of bacon and maple syrup hung in the air by the roadside apartment blocks.

But no one was up yet, reading their paper.

He hurtled up the hill that led to town, dragging a tired Prince beside him. "Sorry, buddy. Being impatient makes my legs go faster. What say I buy us a donut at Sweets and Treats and you can have a tiny, tiny piece."

It was hard to tell what Prince's thoughts were on the matter, because the dog was panting like a steam engine.

"Ha!" he said, startling a middle-aged man in worn boxers who had emerged from his house and was in the process of collecting his newspaper from his dew-soaked lawn. So, someone *was* reading the paper. "Morning," he huffed, and kept on charging up the hill.

The question was, how many residents on Prospect Road were up reading their newspapers?

Andy had promised to text him if Katie turned up at the control tower. Persuading the old fellow to let him into the tower had taken a full set of signed original Anton Price hardbacks, but he'd been happy to part with them. Andy's wife got to be happy with her new books, and he got what he wanted. An opportunity.

He was so busy rethinking his plans, hoping he hadn't forgotten something important, that he didn't remember he'd promised the dog a donut until he'd passed the café and was on the final stretch home. "Let's have some water," he said. "Then we'll walk down. I promise. I need to keep busy today, pal, which means you do too."

He turned into the track that led to his garden gate, and Prince lunged ahead of him, nearly pulling his arm from his socket. "Whoa there, buddy. We use our manners, remember?"

But then he saw what had piqued Prince's attention. Rose the golden retriever was sitting in his garden admiring the ocean view.

And behind her, seated in the sun beside his pot of geraniums, was Katie.

HE LOOKED amazing when he ran. Tall, strong, a little windswept. Like an eighteenth-century warrior who'd shucked off his armor for the day and somehow ended up in high-tech running gear. And this man—this kind, successful, thoughtful man—was into her.

*Her.* Katie Shields, responsible worker, dedicated dog behavioral therapist, and world-class failure at word games.

It seemed too good to be true, which had to be why she

hadn't seen it. She was a logical person. Logical people didn't believe in happy endings where the Hollywood warrior picked the lonely pumpkin.

Wait. She was mixing her metaphors. Where the Hollywood warrior picke—

All thoughts of metaphors slid from her brain as Anton let himself into his garden gate and dropped to the ground beside her. "Katie," he said, breathing hard from his run. "Man, am I glad to see you."

She wasn't sure she knew what to say. How often did a pumpkin get to be wooed so sweetly as Anton had wooed her? The photograph. The words. The velvet box. She held out her hands, and he wrapped them in his.

"You know, I've been daydreaming about this moment for hours," he said, "but in my daydream I was looking a whole lot less sweaty, and more groomed and...er, chiseled."

She snickered. That was what she had needed, a reminder that he may be the love of her life, but he was also her very best friend. "Chiseled? Is that a word they teach you in thriller writing school?"

"Thriller Writing 101. The hero is always chiseled."

She squeezed his hand. "I'm sorry I ran away from you last week."

He squeezed back. "I'm sorry, too."

"I had...some stuff to think through. Stuff that had been building up for a long time. It was getting in the way of me being able to see what was going on around me."

He smiled, a lopsided one that held some of the fear she could feel herself. "Like the overgrown crossword lummox you were hanging out with, who was falling in love with you?"

"Yeah," she said softly. "Like that."

Anton's eyes crinkled at the corners when he looked at her. She loved that.

She loved the way his house was now littered with dog toys and water bowls and chewed-up agapanthus stems, and he didn't care a whit.

His eyes dropped to the velvet box resting on her lap. "You opening that anytime soon?"

"I'm going to, but I think I already know what it says."

He raised his eyebrows. "You have a spy in the Cove and Co. Jewelers?"

She grinned. "You're a funny guy, Price. No. I know what it says because I think I finally understand what you, and Andy, and Veronica, and even my rat of an ex-boyfriend—"

"Who we never need to mention ever again."

"—have been trying to tell me. It's not the words, it's how they're said. It's not the logical one plus one, it's the whole great bubbling mess: mistakes and love and fun and crazy and all of the stuff I've been closing out ever since Uncle Roly died. I tried to pack everything into neat little packages, then closed myself off to life."

"I wish I'd had a chance to meet your uncle."

"Yeah," she said, grateful when he pulled her in close so she could lean her head against his broad, warm chest. "Me too. I think after his funeral, living in his house with Veronica...I transferred my need to be cared for to Vee. It wasn't fair."

"But understandable."

His voice rumbled through his t-shirt when he spoke, through the thin fabric, through the thinner fabric of her blouse, and right into her heart. It helped her find a way to admit how vulnerable she'd been. "When I think of all the upset I caused, just because my adult sister didn't get in touch with me for a week. No wonder the police weren't saddling up a posse when I went to report her as a missing person."

The last time she and Anton had talked about how she had dealt with her sister's absence, she'd pushed him away. Someone she'd loved had told her a truth she was frightened of hearing, and she'd lashed out instead of learning.

*Someone she loved.* She looked up into Anton's dear face. "I think I'm ready to open my box."

"Okay," he said, as Prince and Rose quit their wrestling and lined up on either side of him, sitting up as proudly as groomsmen.

The velvet was the deep blue of the ocean just on dusk. She ran her hands over it, feeling the leather of the underlying box creak as she pried the hinge open.

A ring.

*A ring!*

And not just any old ring, but a ring for her. It was simple and gold, and a stone so clear it caught the sunlight as it flickered up from its satin bed. "It's too perfect to touch," she breathed.

"Allow me," Anton said, and he reached long fingers into the box and pulled out the ring. "I'd kneel, but…" He shrugged and gave her a half smile from his position sitting cross-legged across from her, their knees touching.

"What does it say?" he said, a tremor in his voice as though the sea breeze had stolen some of his strength.

This was her moment. She'd tricked herself into believing that being alone wasn't lonely; that being alone was safer than being hurt again when loved ones left. She'd not understood that without a little risk, she'd never know reward.

Anton had pushed her out of that foolish thinking. He'd

believed in her need to find her sister, he'd supported her, he'd been there and now she knew why. Finally, she understood all the clues he'd thrown her way.

She closed her eyes. "Before I guess what the words on the ring say, I have something to say for myself."

He took a breath. "What?"

"I thought I would be safe from being hurt again if I closed off my heart."

He held her hand. "I know, honey."

"You pried it open. Even though I tried not to let you."

He smiled, a half-grin that would have melted her heart if it hadn't already turned itself into syrup. "I was giving it my all, Katie."

"Your all was my everything. I love you, Anton. And I'm telling you that with my heart wide open."

"Oh, Katie."

He was gathering her to him, but she held him back. There was more she needed to say. "I'm no good at words and games and reading people, I never have been. I'm better at facts than at emotions, which is why I've struggled to trust myself, trust my reactions to people. But with you, Anton, I think I've finally learned to trust myself. To trust you."

She reached her hand toward his and wrapped it around the ring he held. The hard facets of the stone were like the facts she ran her life by, that helped her anchor her emotions. "The engraving of the ring says you love me."

"Read it and see."

She held the ring up to the light and saw a plain script etched into the narrow band. *I love you, Katie.*

"Can I kiss you now?" he said.

"Wait. I haven't apologized yet for being so…"

"Prickly?"

She raised her eyebrows. "Unsure, I was going to say."

"I'm a professional agony aunt, Katie," he said with a grin. "I know prickly when it's running out of my house crying after waffles."

She pursed her lips. "Okay. I'm letting you win this one only because it's true, I have been such an idiot."

He smiled. "I know."

She frowned at him. "You're supposed to say *no, you haven't.*"

He pulled her closer, so their foreheads touched. "I never lie to the women I'm in love with."

"The women you're—"

It was hard to get out the rest of her question, because Anton's mouth had found hers and she briefly forgot about questions and answers, and prickliness and love...all she could do was feel.

LATER, much later, she circled back. "So," she said. "About all these women you're in love with..."

He was sitting beside her on his terrace, his hand around hers where the ring he'd given her glinted in the morning sun. "What's that thing you're always telling me? You're a one-plus-one-equals-two kinda girl?"

"Um, yes?"

He pointed at her. "One."

He pointed at himself. "Plus one. That's my two, Katie, and I'm planning—hoping—on keeping us together forever. With dogs, of course. You okay with that?"

She was so, so okay with that. She leaned her head into his shoulder and breathed him in. "So. Any chance of a waffle?"

"I'm doing B this week. Would a banana fritter interest you at all?"

So long as Anton was the one doing the frittering, she would be very, very interested.

## EPILOGUE

*A*nton had wanted to write their own vows for the wedding, which was an idea Katie supported wholeheartedly...until it came time to write her own.

Sure, he was a celebrity writer, with his new book, *Ghost Quotient*, filling up every bestseller shelf in the country. How hard was it for him to come up with some profound words?

For her, writing vows was more difficult. She didn't have a gift for wordplay or cleverness. But she did love Anton, and that had to be enough.

She looked up at him from beneath the froth of veil Vee had insisted she wear and squeezed Anton's hand for courage.

"I, Katie Shields, promise to love you, Anton Price, always and forever. I promise to hold you close to me every night and laugh with you every day. I promise this to you with my whole heart."

Anton's dark eyes had taken on a shinier luster with every word she spoke. The celebrant gave him a moment, then nodded.

"I, Anton Price," he said, and his voice was rough.

She squeezed his hand. This was big, this vow stuff. But here they were, together, making them. She could hear sniffles from the vicinity immediately behind her and knew that Vee was feeling this as deeply as she was.

He nodded at her, then continued. "I promise to love you, Katie, always and forever. I promise to keep you happy. I promise to trust you when you're quiet, celebrate with you when you're joyful. I promise not to go ballistic when your dog digs up my hydrangeas, and I promise to be honest every day of our lives."

The minister stepped closer. "Katie and Anton, I now pronounce you wife and husband. Anton? You may kiss your bride."

She let him lift the tulle of her veil up over her head. He was smiling at her, and she could hear the murmurs of support from the people crowded into Anton's tiny front garden. Danny and Julia had held hands and cried through the entire wedding service. Vee had arrived with her boyfriend Pete, then proceeded to ignore him and now they stood at opposite ends of the garden. A smattering of Redwood Cove locals were there that she barely knew—yet!—friends of Anton's from school. Andy and Carmelita were busy at the birth of their fourth grandchild and hadn't been able to make it, and Ramon had been weirdly cagey about how busy he might be on the day.

But really? She didn't mind who was there to celebrate with them. Anton was all she needed. Anton, and their four-legged support crew, who had behaved impeccably despite the quantity of salmon crepes being passed around by the catering staff.

"Your first kiss as Mrs. Price," he murmured. "You ready?"

She breathed in. "So ready, Mr. Price. Show me what you've got."

And yeah. He showed her.

ANTON GLANCED at Katie as he pulled the Jeep off the highway and turned onto the rough gravel track. He'd left the Jeep's cover off, so her sun-streaked hair was rippling wildly in the breeze.

Almost, he thought with a grin, as wildly as the ears of their backseat passengers. Rose was perched behind him, sitting up like a princess being taken on an outing to wave at her loyal subjects. Prince, on the other hand—despite his regal name—had his tongue out, and his wild black hair was a tangled mess.

A phone trilled, and Katie pulled her mobile from the purse at her feet. "It's Vee," she said. "Do you mind? It's probably some wedding related drama. The caterers can't find their check, perhaps. Or maybe Danny's still crying, and she doesn't know how to handle it."

He grinned. Letting Vee run the wedding aftermath so he and Katie could make a run for it had been a genius move, if he said so himself. "Go for it."

"Hi," she said into her phone. "You *what?*"

He couldn't hear much of what Veronica was saying but it seemed to need a lot of *oh no* and *I'm so sorry* comments from Katie. When she hung up, she turned to him. "Pete broke up with her."

He winced. "At our wedding? Ouch. How's she doing?"

"She's in the angry-crying stage. Everyone's gone home,

and she says she's going to bury herself in your den and binge-watch *Steel Magnolias,* followed by every Hallmark Christmas movie she can find."

"Boy. That is so going to mess up my suggested viewing algorithms."

She laughed. "Not something she will care about right now. She also says she's found your bourbon stash, and she'll replace anything she smashes."

He raised his eyebrows. "Um…should we be worried?"

"No. This is normal. I'll call her tomorrow and see how upset she is."

"Sure." Because he was pretty sure he wasn't interrupting his honeymoon for anything.

He flicked his turn signal and turned off the road onto an even narrower track, then drove the Jeep along at slow speed for a few yards. A string of maples formed a long, red-brown avenue of autumn color as he followed the track into a drive-way, then he brought the Jeep to a stop in a patch of fresh-mown grass before a neat log cabin.

Trees dotted rough-mown fields, and to their right, squatted a long barn with bright red doors.

"Wait," Katie said. "I thought our mystery honeymoon was a five-hour drive away. Is this it? We only just left Redwood Cove."

He grinned. "About that. I was employing a Thriller Writing 101 strategy known as misdirection. We're having a small detour on the way to our honeymoon."

"We are?"

She was looking about, and even though he'd seen the place before, he got an extra thrill out of watching Katie see it for the first time.

"This place is gorgeous, Anton. Who lives here? A friend of yours?"

This was the moment where he found out if she was going to be okay with him muscling in on her therapy gig. A screen door slapped open, and he looked up. "Oh good. He's here."

"Who's h—is that *Ramon?*"

"Ant, my man. Katie. Good to see you both."

The barks from the back seat were starting to deafen him, so he reached back and unclipped the dogs' harnesses so they could bound to the ground.

Katie was looking at him, wide-eyed.

"Confession time," he said. "When I adopted Prince from the refuge, I asked Ramon what his ideal place would be to house the dogs they were working to rehome."

She gasped. "You bought this place?"

"Yeah. Well, I had all those royalties from that book that had been weighing on my conscience for a year, so I decided I could do something more useful with them than whining about them. I bought this place, and I'm leasing it to the refuge center."

"For a dollar a month," said Ramon.

"Anton," Katie said, and when her eyes filled with tears, he knew he needn't have worried.

"Danny and Jules have agreed to come out and do a news piece about the important work the refuge does, and Ramon thinks he can get a fundraising page up to help fit out the barn with kennels and a hydrobath, that sort of thing."

"Ramon, I cannot believe you kept this from me. Wait— was this why you didn't come to our wedding? You were setting up a new refuge?"

He shrugged. "Guilty as charged. You wanna say your vows again in front of me, go nuts."

"Once was perfect," she said, sliding her hand into Anton's. "It is amazing." She turned to him. "You are amazing."

"It's true," he said, grinning. "But now my amazingness has found a purpose. What shall we call this place?"

She groaned. "Oh heavens, not an anagram, I'm begging you."

"Whatever you like." He'd found a purpose for his royalties. He'd found Katie. So long as he could keep her, anything else was a bonus.

"I've got their beds, Anton. Two weeks of supplies. Me and Rose and Prince are going to have a fine old time."

Katie swiveled her head towards him, and he shrugged. "You happy if Ramon dog sits for us?"

"Anton Price. Just how much more have you not told me?"

He grinned. "That's it, I promise." He waited until Ramon's attention had been distracted by the dogs, then gathered Katie into his arms. "You sure you don't mind me doing this?"

She rested her hand on his cheek. "Of course I'm sure. Anton, I don't know how to thank you."

"I don't need thanks, ever. I just need to know you're happy."

She smiled up at him. "So happy, Anton."

He tucked his arm under hers and set off to show her the five shady acres he'd bought. Keeping Katie happy was a vow he'd never break.

## THE END

## STELLA QUINN'S BOOKS
### ROMANCE | ADVENTURE | ESCAPE

*Please leave a review if you get the chance (on any book distributors website, or on GoodReads) - it makes such a difference to us writers. Thank you x*

*TURN THE PAGE TO READ THE FIRST CHAPTER OF TROPIC STORM*

**What readers have said**

"X-factor nailed it. You can start bidding wars with this."

"I want to buy the trilogy – actually, I want you as my new best friend."

"Wonderful voice and loved your humor."

"Really enjoyed these characters."

**The Island Escape Series**

Romance and drama on sun-dazzled beaches - the heroines are fun and the heroes are heart-throbs, why not escape with them on your own vacation romance?

Prequel novella: And I Always Will (Charlotte & Jack)
Book 1: Tropic Storm (Charlotte & Jack)
Book 2: Stowaway (Sabrina & Ben)
Book 3: Island Fling (Antonia & Tyler)
Christmas novella: Catching Snow (Lisa & Ryan)

～

### *The Clementine Springs Series*

Small town romance set in Upstate New York - horses and steamboats, country music stars and lakes, why not head escape the crisp mountain air and discover love again?

Spring novella: *The Umbrella Diaries* (Marianne & Duncan)
Christmas novella: *All I Want* (Prudence & Adam)
*Summer Loving* (Leila & Damon)

### *Other Books*

*Christmas on Hope Street (an anthology)*

To chat, and hear about new releases, and all things Stella, why not join my reader team!
Subscribe at www.stellaquinnauthor.com/subscribe

For books without links here, head on over to my webpage for up-to-date information: www.stellaquinnauthor.com

SNEAKY PEAK ...

FIRST CHAPTER OF TROPIC STORM, THE
ISLAND ESCAPE SERIES

Charlotte Jones paused amid the crowded departure lounge of Los Angeles International Airport. Shining up at her from the display rack at the front of an airport shop was the familiar cover of Bella magazine. But was it the latest issue?

She broke into a grin as she pulled the glossy magazine out of its stand. Her last article had made the cover, she hadn't expected that. A dancer slumped on a backstage prop, all heels and legs and bling, her oversize feathers discarded on the floor beside her. Charlotte ran a finger over the dancer's weary face, the loud pop of color from the flamingo pink of the feather. The photographer had nailed it this time.

"You buying that, lady? You wanna library, you're gonna have to go someplace else."

"Relax, I'm buying," she said and placed the magazine down on the counter. She'd have a copy waiting for her when she returned home to London, stuffed into her mailbox and wrapped in a yard of bio-degradable plastic, but why wait? She'd never got over the thrill of seeing her freelance articles in print, and she had a six-hour flight ahead of her. She'd be able to read the magazine cover to cover.

"A bottle of water too, thanks."

She rifled through the pound notes in her purse until she found her clip of American money, then handed a ten dollar note to the rumpled man at the till. Leaving the change on the counter, she headed back into the flow of people and cast a look upward to the screens. The letters clicked over on a departure board, white font over a black background: Hawaiian Airlines to Honolulu, terminal 5, gate 58.

A thrum of anticipation joined the jitters in her chest. This was more than a holiday about to start, this was a one-woman retreat, just for her, a journey towards peace, solitude, well-being. She crossed her fingers, pinkie promised herself that it would work. As much as she loved her job writing opinion pieces in magazines, and her hobby-slash-obsession writing for her women's issues blog, she needed to recover before going on assignment again. She closed her eyes, and imagined the sunshine, saltwater and sea breezes soothing her jangled nerves. Hawaii and happiness ... she couldn't wait.

The queue to enter the waiting lounge at her gate was snaking down the corridor by the time she made her way through the sprawling airport. Couples leaned on each other, taking selfies to pass the time, children squealed and bounced with excitement. An elderly woman wearing pearls the size of mothballs was having a heated discussion with a check-in attendant about the size of her carry-on luggage.

Charlotte smiled. People, chatter, hustle-and-bustle: she'd forgotten how much she used to enjoy the chaos of travel. And today, despite the crowds, she felt good. She felt strong, for the first time in months. Perhaps her psychologist was right, and she really would recover. There'd been days when she'd wondered if she'd be trapped by stress forever. How would she work then?

A tinny voice from overhead broke her train of thought. Just as well – now was not the time to be dwelling on what had happened to her in Barwick three months ago.

*Passengers on flight HA4 to Honolulu, your plane has been delayed. Please remain near the departure gate and await further instruction.*

A collective groan issued from the people queued about her, and she shuffled forward with them through the security check. She'd spent a lot of time in airport lounges over the years. What was an hour or two more?

She slung her leather carry-all on to the conveyor belt, showed her passport and ticket to the check-in attendant and was waved through to the dubious comfort of the holding area. At least there were seats available. She chose a plastic chair by the window and settled in to wait, rolling her shoulders to relax some of the kinks. It had been a long flight over from London, and she was tired.

A toddler nearby broke into a wail, breaking her train of thought. Flashing a look over to the departure screen to check how long she was going to be trapped in a seat next to a young person with lungs the size of Texas, her gaze fell on a dark-suited figure entering the lounge and all thoughts of kinked muscles fled from her brain.

"Oh, my," she muttered.

A handsome man was walking through the security screening area. She studied him covertly over her magazine. Six foot one, she decided, skimming the length of him from his close cropped, dark blond hair to his expensively shod feet. His suit was the darkest grey, emphasizing the white of his collar and cuffs, and the body it covered left Charlotte's lips forming an *oh* of admiration. She wondered what color his eyes were, then turned resolutely to her magazine.

She'd never been lucky where men were concerned, no matter what their eye color, so really, what was the point in looking? She flipped through the glossy pages to her article. Bella Magazine had been her first serious job, back when she'd thought being an investigative reporter in war torn countries would be a great way to prove to the world that she had made something of herself. Luckily for her, she'd been to school for a time with the magazine's news editor. Antonia still contracted her for the odd article, which helped keep the funds flowing in. And this latest one had been a delight to write. It wasn't her usual piece – she was more at home advising women on ways to hop, skip and jump over the gender pay gap, or reviewing the latest mindfulness apps bombarding the market – but something about the chorus girls in London's latest stage show had appealed to her. The hard graft behind the glamour, the sweat beneath the sequins ... she had found something when she interviewed the dancers which had resonated. The drive to succeed came at a price. For the dancers, it was the injuries, the uncertainty of work ahead, the competition for work within a shrinking industry.

Charlotte knew about paying a price for success. She'd spent the last decade paying it.

The toddler's wail reached a pitch capable of shattering bullet-proof glass, and she cast a glance about, wondering if it would be too obvious if she changed seats. Oh, yes! There was one free, and oh-happy-day it was right next to Mr. Hot Suit.

She glanced up at his face only to encounter him looking back at her with shocked recognition. Oh my god. No, it couldn't be. She dropped her eyes to the magazine she held in her hand, and felt heat rushing up through her cheeks.

*Jack.*

The calm she had been feeling, the happy puff of anticipation about starting her holiday, evaporated. Her hands gripped the *Bella* issue as though it was a shield. Why did it have to be Jack?

She peeled her fingers off the magazine, noting how clammy her palms had become. She had to calm the hell down. Finding herself in the same departure lounge as the man who had smashed her world to smithereens nine years ago ... it was too much. Maybe she could have dealt with it calmly if she wasn't already a mess about the fiasco in Barwick. But the fiasco had happened, and she was all out of bravery.

She kept her eyes averted, knowing she was behaving like a big chicken, but unable to help herself. Hopefully he'd have the decency to stay well away from her. She did not know if she could handle a confrontation with the man she had once been foolish enough to lose her heart to.

*Ladies and gentlemen,* a voice blared from the speaker above her head, *we are pleased to announce flight HA4 to Honolulu is now ready for boarding.*

Oh, thank god. The airline companies fit three hundred people on these planes – with luck, they'd be seated well away from each other. She had an eye mask in her bag, ear plugs. She'd wrap an airline blanket around her head if she had to. She could not face Jack. Not now, not ever.

She slung her bag over her shoulder, checking her belongings were all safely tucked away, then rose to her feet. She marched to the boarding gate, checked her pass, then took off down the long airbridge to the plane. Fast walking was *not* running. Charlotte Jones did *not* run away.

"Well, not often," she admitted to herself as she sank into the plush comfort of her seat. She closed her eyes and willed her heartbeat to settle into a calmer cadence.

Her phone buzzed, and she reached to silence it. The words *Antonia is calling* scrolled over the glass screen. She sighed. Antonia wasn't just the editor of Bella magazine – she'd have ended the call if she was, future work prospects be damned. Antonia was also one of her oldest friends and was not the sort of person you could ignore, even from half a world away.

She lifted the phone to her ear and braced herself for the onslaught.

"Charlotte, have you arrived? Tell me everything. Is the water warm? Are the cocktails cold? Wait. Any single guys? You know I've got weeks of holiday owing; I can be there like a shot if there's single guys."

Nothing changed. She smiled. "Toni, I'm nowhere near Hawaii. I'm parked on a tarmac in the States. No cocktail umbrellas in sight."

"Bummer. Call me the instant you get to the hotel, won't you? I'll worry if you don't."

"Yes, matron."

"None of that cheek from you, young lady. But seriously, how are you coping with the crowds? No dramas in the airports? No panicky whatsits?"

She closed her eyes, and a vision of the grey-suited drama called Jack came into view. "Not that sort of drama, no."

There was a pause. Charlotte imagined her friend's brain scrambling through the innuendo of that remark. She chuckled to herself at Toni's next words.

"Tell. Me. Everything."

She let out a breath. Was she ready to talk about it? She sighed and took the plunge. "You'll never guess the man I just saw at LAX."

"Umm. A Hemsworth? Hugh Grant? Colin Firth?"

"Somebody I actually know."

There was a pause. "I'm struggling here, Charlotte. You live like a nun. Do you even know any men? I can't think of a single one you've given tuppence about since Jack bloody Diamond back when you were a cadet journalist in London, and I was backpacking my way through the single men of Europe."

The silence stretched out as Charlotte waited for the penny to drop. Or tuppence, in this case.

"Holy crap. You're not seriously telling me you ran into Jack Diamond?"

"Yep. The rat himself."

"I'm speechless."

Charlotte laughed. "Well, that's a first."

"So, what happened?"

"I ran away."

"Ran away? You? Charlotte the bad-ass women-are-champions blogging queen?"

She could hardly believe it herself. But the heart was a tender thing, and she'd forgotten how tender hers could feel. "It was actually pretty tough seeing him, Toni."

She could hear her friend's nails tapping on a hard surface.

Antonia was at work, no doubt ripping adverbs from some hapless reporter's article.

"Yeah, I bet," Antonia said at last. "Listen, Charlotte, I have to take a call from Barcelona, but we should talk this out. Oh, and you know that draft article you gave me? The one on the Barwick riots?"

Oh yeah, she knew that one alright. She'd written it up in her hospital bed while under the influence of a surfeit of common-sense-dulling drugs. Well, she hadn't so much as written it as dictated it into her phone, as her arm had been buried within six inches of plaster. Thousands of words on the women's issues blogger who'd been on her way to a café to interview a woman about a community gardening project, but instead found herself in the middle of a riot that swept through the regional city when police shot a man in the street.

She regretted having written it now – she'd been too raw, too deeply affected to be objective in her reporting. Antonia could bin it, that was fine. "Don't worry about the article, I shouldn't have sent it in."

"Don't worry about it? Girlfriend, it is fantastic. I've entered it into the press awards. It's taking center stage in the next issue of Bella."

"Antonia—" She drifted to a close. Thinking about that day still had the power to upset her. She'd not be reading the article when it was published.

She heard her friend sigh down her end of the phone. "Charlotte. We don't have to talk about this now, forget I mentioned it, okay? Why don't you skype me when you're settled in Hawaii? I'll invite Sabrina over to my place, and the three of us can bitch about men and bossy editors until you get that sad little sound out of your voice. I don't like hearing it."

Charlotte smiled. Bossy or not, Antonia was as fabulous as a friend could be. "It's a date. And thanks."

She slipped her phone over into airplane mode and dropped it into her bag. She was lucky to have Antonia and Sabrina in her life, and she knew it. Her old school chums had been there for her through the high moments and the low.

The muted hubbub of the filling plane was comfortingly familiar. She turned to her window and gazed across the vacant seat through to the busy airstrip. Only a few more hours until her holiday started. The website for the hotel she had booked promised perfection. Part of the Jewel Resort Group, the Jewel of Oahu was set amid lush Hawaiian gardens, with views spanning a perfect beach and the Pacific Ocean beyond.

She sank into a daydream of bathing in sun-dappled water and lying in the feathered shade of coconut palms. She could think about the project her psychologist had been encouraging her to pursue, or maybe read the half-dozen books she had included in her luggage. She smiled. Would she read the romcom first? Or the new thriller that—

"Excuse me."

Charlotte opened her eyes and sat up, reaching out an instinctive hand to smooth her wayward auburn hair. Oh no. Fate couldn't be so cruel.

"If you wouldn't mind letting me past so I can get to my seat," Jack said.

"Of course," she muttered, rising to her feet. And she'd better get her wits together while she was at it.

She stepped out into the aisle of the plane, her gaze locked on to his. He was even more impressive than she remembered. Her breath caught and she felt a surge of heat travel through her until even her fingertips tingled. She pressed herself against the seat on the other side of the aisle to widen the gap between the man who had broken her heart and her afflicted senses.

Jack stowed his briefcase and brushed past Charlotte in the narrow confines of the airplane corridor. His suit coat dragged at the linen of her dress, and she breathed in his scent, a clean warm smell overlaid with a whisper of cologne. She gripped her fingers into the worn fabric of the plane seat and forced herself to look away. Any view would be preferable to watching Jack slide past her just inches away.

She waited a beat, then risked a glance sideways.

Jack was seated. She could do this. She could blank him out for the next few hours the way she'd been blanking him out for the last decade. Schooling her features into a neutral expression, she sank once more into her seat, giving him a cool nod.

He raised an eyebrow and held out his hand. "It's been a long time," he said. His American accent reminded her of their differences.

"Has it?" She wanted very badly to ignore that outstretched hand, but pride had her reaching out to shake it. Why give him the satisfaction of learning how flustered she was?

His warm hand closed briefly around hers. Memories of those long fingers and how they felt against her skin crashed through her thoughts. Blanking him out for the last decade hadn't been enough; she should have tried harder. Hypnotism. Therapy. Exorcism. She was saved from having to indulge in further conversation by the arrival of an in-flight steward bearing a tray of drinks.

"We haven't seen you for a while, Mr. Diamond," said the steward.

Jack helped himself to a glass of water. "Work's been keeping me in the States lately, Graeme. How's life in the skies treating you?"

First name basis with the cabin crew? Jack must be a regular on the flight to Honolulu. She had forgotten he had grown up there. Well, not so much forgotten, as forced herself to forget. She helped herself to a glass of champagne and nodded her thanks to the steward. Jetlag, fatigue, lack-of-sleep – her travel was catching up with her, and she took a large sip to steady her jangling nerves. How on earth was she going to survive the next six hours?

If only he'd grown bald and smelly. Or was travelling with a plump wife and screaming toddler triplets in tow and had carrot puree mushed into the front of his suit. Her eyes shot a look over to his left hand before she could prevent them. No ring. Not that she cared. But still – there was no denying it, he was better looking now than the day she had last seen him, when he'd leapt into a taxi and taken off to Heathrow Airport and left her outraged and crying on the curb.

How gullible she had been. How utterly, stupidly foolish to think he had been any different from her parents, from the world. Charlotte closed her eyes against the sting of unshed tears. She would not let this man know how much she still hurt. Pride was all that had kept her going after Jack sauntered out of her life. Her pride and her career. She was damned if she would be losing that too, after all this time.

She could barely remember the girl she had been. An

idealist, a dreamer, all enthusiasm and passion and no wisdom. How ironic: she, who'd vowed to forge a career from words and make her living investigating the deeper truths of an issue, had just crawled into a hole of misery when Jack left. She'd not hunted him down and forced him to return. She'd not beaten a path to his door and wedged herself there until he'd explained why a big-buck salary on the far side of the world was more important than her. She'd been too hurt.

Too young, she acknowledged.

She was not that young, foolish girl now. If she weren't feeling so vulnerable after the incident in Barwick, maybe this could have been an opportunity to question the ghosts of her past, and finally let them rest. But she *was* vulnerable. This time, she had to put herself first, which meant the last thing she needed was to complicate her much needed holiday. She would find out where he was headed, so she could avoid any further accidental meetings.

Fueling her courage with the last inch of her champagne, she laid a hand on the arm of his chair.

*… want to keep reading? Tropic Storm (The Island Escape Series) is available at all your favourite retailers, in print and ebook format.*

www.ingramcontent.com/pod-product-compliance
Lightning Source LLC
Chambersburg PA
CBHW020138120726
47903CB00007B/2318